going to the
mountain

Some of the stories in this volume have appeared in Epoch, North American Review, Paris Review *and* Black Ice.

This project is in part supported by grants from the National Endowment for the Arts in Washington, D.C., a federal agency, and the Charles Phelps Taft Memorial Fund, University of Cincinnati.

Library of Congress Cataloging-in-Publication Data
Wiebe, Dallas E.
    Going to the mountain.
    Contents: Going to the mountain — At the rotonde — Night flight to Stockholm — (etc.).
    I. Title.
PS3573.I3G6   1988   813'.54   87-25627
ISBN 0-930901-49-5 (pbk.)
ISBN 0-930901-50-9 (pbk., signed)

Dallas Wiebe

GOING TO THE MOUNTAIN

BURNING DECK, PROVIDENCE

Contents

Going to the Mountain

REMEMBER HOW HAPPY I was the day I was born because I was anxious to get started writing things down. While drifting about in my mom's water and tethered to her by a battledore placenta I couldn't record things because I had no pen and paper and no dictionary to check spellings. As my head emerged, I looked about to see if I was near a stationery store. I wasn't, so just as soon as the pain subsided from the Asian swat that knocked the crap out of my ears, nose, eyes and mouth I said to dad, "You're Jonathan David Prick. Get me a tablet and a ballpoint pen." My dad looked at me, drew back his fist and said, "Watch your mouth, you little creep." Mom, Mary Beth Bigger Than A Barn, grabbed his arm and said to me, "Why did you call him that?" "Well," I said, "that's what you always call him." It was the beginning of a difficult life.

I don't know exactly when I first had thoughts. I don't know when I first heard human voices. My mom took a lot of drugs while I was ceasing to be a fish and often I would spin about like a trapeze artist and hear voices saying, "Give me another blue" and "I don't think you should take that in your condition." The boundaries of my pristine consciousness were often obfuscated by a chemical imperative. What I do know is that I remember everything I've ever heard, thought or known. I haven't forgotten a thing from the first vague voices I heard while I did jazzercise in the amniotic fluid to the foreign voice saying, "Just relax, miss," from the dark finger poking around just outside my pool to the rubber gloves over my ears as I formulated my first written sentence. My head feels bloated because of the burden of remembering so much, and now I have to face Kindergarten.

When I was laid at my mother's side for the first time, my pulse was 132.4, my temperature 103.1, me worrying about my omphalorrhexis, her breath was so bad I tried to hold my breath. I couldn't because dad was tickling the sole of my left foot. I wailed out, "Dad, for Krishna's sake, cut the crap." He did and I sucked in some foul wind and started to turn puce. My mom called for Doctor Creep Who Won't Go Back to India, who came and said, "What is the matter, Miss Navel?" My dad jumped out of his chair, stuck the earplugs of Punjab's stethoscope back into those dark ears and yelled into the end of it, "Our name is Nevil, not Navel. And if you don't get it right, I'll make you eat sacred cowshit." Doctor Miasma Gandhi said, "Please lower your voice. You'll wake up your relatives in the zoo." My sweating dad yelled, "Listen, Gunga Din, you say one more word and I'll stick your rupees right up your New Delhi." Dr. Dark-Skinned Idiot smiled at me and said softly, "I'm from Lahore." My dad, as I expected, because I was already measuring his intelligence and his language and I was listening closely so that as soon as I could get the ballpoint pen and some paper I was going to write it all down, came back with what I already knew he was going to say and what I was never going to be able to forget. My mother sighed, a horrible stench rushed over me, I breathed out and my pulse went to 136.5 and my temperature to 104.2.

(My memory is hot. My mind is shaking.) My dad, Jonathan David Naval — our name really is Naval — is a professor of English at Miami University in Oxford, Ohio. He doesn't know much, but he reads a lot and he likes to use big phrases like "The burden of the past." Which he used, and which I remembered, on the first day of my nursing. I was sucking my mom's left jug when I heard J.D. say, "Now we will experience the burden of the past." I looked up from that fuchsia nipple I was gnawing on and asked him if that had anything to do with "The Significance of the Frontier in American History." Professor Naval Base said, "Where did you hear about that?" I said he had talked about it to mom when I was four months, eight days, fifteen

hours, four minutes and twenty-five seconds old and
my temperature was 102.9 and my pulse was 132.1.
I heard that just after I heard through the tube that
mom was wearing a chartreuse negligee that cost
$14.82. I remember that it was the biggest one dad
could get but mom couldn't get it down over her
belly so dad told her to wear it around her neck
and to go to hell if she wasn't satisfied with it because he had looked all over the K Mart and it took
him three hours and thirteen minutes to find it and
he spent thirty-four minutes in the checkout line and
when he came out he had a flat tire, left rear, on his
Dodge Omni.

After I emptied Mary Beth's jugs, dad and I
discussed Frederick Jackson Turner. He explained
how Turner's thesis was first published in 1894
and how important it was in regard to manifest
destiny, the rise of the middle class and the leap of
faith. I asked him about progress and poverty, Ver-
itism, Horatio Alger, Jr., native American realism,
free-soilers, the revolt of the masses and the sleep of
reason. The next day he brought me a long biblio-
graphy and told me that I could go, as soon as I was
up and about, to the King Library and check out the
books. He said he'd get me an office in Bachelor Hall
right next to his so that he could come in and remove the books from the tray on my highchair as
soon as I'd finished reading them. He said the other
faculty members wouldn't like it but that I shouldn't
worry because they were just a bunch of schmucks.

For my first birthday, Dr. J.D. Naval Reconnais-
sance gave me a copy of *Crime and Punishment*, in

Russian, so I could read it while I was being toilet
trained. I'd already read all of Flaubert in French,
Cervantes in Spanish, Homer in Greek. The King
Library was about out of stuff I wanted to read. Of
course, all that reading was multiplying all the things
I remembered and could not forget. Mary Beth
bought me some glasses at the K Mart and I took
care of Raskolnikov in one day. Dad said he was
glad my birthday didn't come everyday. I recited to
him all the phone numbers of all the people in Oxford
and he said that we could never move to another
town. I recalled for him all the football scores of all
the Miami Redskins games, the rosters, the weather,
the plays, and he told me that that was another reason why football should be abolished.

I never got that room next to my dad's office. I
stayed in my own room on the second floor of our
house on the road to Hueston Woods where we had
moved because dad's colleagues told him he'd better
move out of town or they were going to burn him
out. My days were filled with reading, writing, remembering. I spun the mobile over my crib and
passed back into what I was and what I had been. I
waited for the seven camel bells attached to my door
to ring when Mary Beth would bring in my meals.
Little jars of apple sauce, ground-up carrots, prunes
squashed to mush. Beech-Nut and Gerber's. Glasses
of milk. Four hundred and twenty-eight and one
half glasses last year. Mary Beth wanting to read me
nursery rhymes and sing little kiddy songs. I listened and meditated on *Das Kapital* and *Ursprungs-
geschichte des Bewusstseins*. Jack and Jill went up

the hill while I waited for Naval Maneuvers to come
home with *War and Peace.* The mountain brook
flowed swift down from its rocky nook and the sun
shined in through the curtains with Mickey Mouse,
Daffy Duck and Porky Pig on them. At night, while
Naval Gunnery and Old Mother Hubbard slept, I
paced the floor and meditated terror. By day I fed
my head. I tied a rope to the light fixture and tried
to spin through the light. I waited for the big dark
finger to shove me around. I put my ear to the
door and knew that soon I would have to shove
my way through it. I looked out the crack in the
door and heard Mother Goose and Naval Disaster
whispering things like, "It's time we did something"
and "He will just have to adjust."

(I wonder if I can remember everything exactly
as it was.) In those formative years I kept my head
to the crack and listened to the voices floating in.
I kept my head to the crack and inhaled the sweet
smoke drifting up from the faculty parties down-
stairs. I circled up along the ceiling. I kicked out in
my mental trapeze. I sat by the window and watched
the moon spin through the sky until Mary Beth
or Naval Station would come in to say good night
and then walk out and fall down the stairs. Those
were the bad moments because Mary Beth would
say, her foul breath washing over me, "Good night,
peachy pie," and I'd answer, "Les sanglots longs/Des
violons/De l'automne" or "Von fern die Uhren
schlagen,/Es ist schon tiefe Nacht." If Dr. Sikh was
at the party, he'd come in and say things like, "There

must be spaces in our togetherness" or "Four men on a bicycle are the army of Buddha." Perhaps not bad things to say, but they knew, or should have known, that I would never forget anything they said. Over and over it came to me that if everything I said was remembered I'd keep my stupid mouth shut. The commitment of ideas to oral articulation must carry with it a categoric responsibility to make sense. Even I, with my ears and nose to the crack, knew that and I was only two years, eight months, nineteen days, twelve hours, sixteen minutes and forty-two seconds old when I thought of it and my pulse was 131.9 and my temperature 102.6 The moon was gibbous, Orion was at forty-five degrees above the eastern horizon and I saw Sirius shining through the woods or else one of my parents' guests, trying to drive home, couldn't find the driveway, as often happened, and the guest would later stagger in and yell, "Who put that god-damned tree in the middle of the road?"

(I must not pause here even though my brain is trembling with memory.) When I was three years old, wise beyond my years and wet behind the ears and elsewhere, walking and practicing tennis against my closed door, doing handstands and cartwheels, lifting weights and doing yoga, Dr. Mowgli took my temperature (102.5) and my pulse (131.2) and told me that someday I would have to descend the stairs and go outside. It was a thought that had not occurred to me but I have never forgotten it. When he said that to me, I wept like a baboon. I felt the sickness unto death and the temptations to suicide. I wondered why I was ever born. I wondered what my place in the universe might be. Dr. Himalaya used cotton balls to wipe away my tears. He untied the rope from the light fixture on the ceiling and told me a story that I will never forget. He said that in Qizil Jilga there is a red panda. He is worshipped by all the bears. The bears come from all over the Himalayas just to smell his odor trail. They come in chariots pulled by snow leopards. They worship the panda and follow him to the headwaters of the Indus River. After the red panda bathes in the stream, the bears drink the water, in fact, they have to empty the stream, which is not easy. When the stream is emptied, the bears put the panda in a cave in the shaking mountain and put a stone in front of the entrance. The bears then fall asleep for the Winter. When a year has passed and the sun again strikes the rock in front of the cave, the stone rolls away, the panda emerges and the bears awaken. Except that now the panda is a boy with a beaked nose and green eyes. The boy remembers everything. He tells the bears where they live so they can return home until the panda comes again. The boy begins to grow red hair. He weeps and wants to go back into the cave, but it is shut to him. He cannot return to the cave. Because the cave doesn't exist. The trembling mountain doesn't exist. Nothing exists except the boy and his way. Dr. Mysore said the moral of the story was that the cave and the rope are one, the wind and the mind are one, the racket and the tennis ball are one, and all these things are multiple.

Twenty-eight days, fourteen hours, twenty-two minutes and fifty-five seconds ago mom carried me out of my room. It was my first trip out of my world since I was brought into it against my will. Mom blindfolded me and carried me down the stairs while I hoped she wouldn't fall. She said she had to take me to the K Mart to buy me something called "school clothes." I remember only the sound of the Omni, the motor clacking, the tires squiggling along the road, the sound of mom sucking on something, the sweet smell filling my oneness. In the K Mart, she put me in a wire cart, removed my blindfold and pushed me around. I could see at my leisure. I looked and I saw and I recorded and I remembered. Green plastic guns. Green garden hoses. Red wagons. Plastic tricycles, red, yellow and pink. Prescription suicide kits. Rolls of barbed deciduate placenta. The colors that came over me like flocks of passenger pigeons. The shapes that ran amok like herds of impala. Racks of candy bars that spilled into my memory like tsunamis over Hokkaido. Frames full of shirts, racks full of underclothes, sneakers by the bushel. My pulse was 131.1 and my temperature 102.3. Cyrillic advertisements, labels in Arabic, Cuneiform guarantees, pidgin English aisle signs, sign language check-out girls, parking attendants speaking Tennessee. Mom sweating in sympathy. Me babbling in short-throat. The eighty-two pistons in our Omni keening out onto the expressway. Two thousand miles per hour into Oxford. Overload. Incoherent cutovers. Maelstrom data. Pinwheel centrifuge.

The inside of my skull lined with pits. I rested for a fortnight while Naval Reserve bathed me with Murine in the eyes, vaseline on the tongue, iodine in the ears, hydrogen peroxide over my medulla oblongata.

Professor Naval Escort said that what I was experiencing was poetry. Dr. Nehru, the Monkey Worshipper, said that the lion who sleeps in his bone is like the whale in a suitcase. Dad said that the whirligig of the thymus is like the stereopticon of the cells. Dr. Bhagavad Gita said that he who stands in a bucket should beware the monkey's uncle. Pop said that the Mississippi River is the aorta of God. Dr. Alien Resident said, "It is said by the sages that the spice under the lion's tongue is the aphrodisiac of the bells." Dad, bless his heart, said, "Skyblue says, 'God created anarchy when he made the duck-billed platypus.' " Dr. Punkah, M.D. to be, glared about and said, "The Master said that white teeth come from eating your enemies." Dad came back, "Skyblue says, 'The Ganges is the piss of swine.' " Calcutta, the temperature-taker, the dispenser of aspirins, the receiver of Medicaid payments, the unmember of the A.M.A., the husband of a woman who can't read the arrows in parking lots because she can't see over the dashboard because she's so fat from having so many kids paid for by American tax dollars, whispered, "Adam and Eve were Hindus." Dad sneered, "The Prophet Mohammad was a Southern Baptist." The snake doctor whispered back, "Billy Graham is from Karachi." Dad: "Madame Nehru sings at the Grand Ole Opry." You've seen a pup chew on a rubber bone. That's the way dad was. Dr. Traitor to His Country stalked out when pop — oh boy was he great — said slowly and with all the majesty of a Ph.D. from Ohio State University (Summa sine Laude), "Ravi Shankar is a disease." When the door slammed shut, dad bellowed through the keyhole, "And penicillin won't cure it."

I said to my dad, "If that was poetry, what should I expect next?" He said next would come philosophy, religion, music, mathematics, art, and fear and trembling. He said that if I feared and trembled enough I might someday know wisdom. I asked him what the difference was between wisdom and philosophy and he said that wisdom makes sense. I wrote it all down and thought about it, thoughts I knew I would never forget. I lay in my crib with the mobile over my face. My mom had made it for "her baby" while I was skindropping and doing my tumbling exercises inside her fetal sack. I remember dad telling her to have seven animals because seven is the number of wholeness and to hang them on three wires because three is the number of dramatic tension. He told her that they could inculcate — that's his word; they probably thought I didn't know what it meant — Freitag's Triangle at an early age. On one wire a duck-billed platypus and a dik-dik. On the second, a dead mackerel, a bluebird and a housefly. On the third, a lamb and a lion. Turning slowly over my green eyes and beaked nose. Turning slowly while I counted the revolutions that I would never forget.

It reminded me of a debate I had imagined between Nietzsche and Gertrude Stein. It reminded me of a conversation I imagined between Henry James and Cervantes. It made me imagine a theory that my crib and a classroom must be alike. It caused me to realize that memory and mountains are alike in that they're just the same on the other side.

My second trip out of my room happened just seven days, three hours, fifty-nine seconds ago. I was four years, 358 days, fourteen hours and nineteen seconds old. My pulse was 128.4 and my temperature 101.8. Dr. Naval Convoy told me it was time for me to again see something other than through a glass window darkly. They blindfolded me so that the shock wouldn't be too great when I underwent poetry for a second time. Dad carried me to the Omni and we drove towards Cincinnati to see dad's old friend, Skyblue the Badass, a.k.a., Peter Solomon Seiltanzer, Professor of English at the University of Cincinnati.

(I must write this all down.) When we reached a place called Millville, mom removed my blindfold. I was looking at a sign: "Millville/Birthplace of Judge Kenesaw Mountain Landis/First Baseball Commissioner." I asked mom to put the blindfold back on, but she said I'd have to put that in my memory — as if I had a choice. The rest of the trip was like that. My brain working at top speed to perceive and record the cars we passed, the license plate numbers, the size of the tires, the occupants of the cars. The number of rows of cabbage in gardens. The clothes on washlines. The dead animals along the way. When I saw places where the ground rose up, I asked mom if those were mountains. She said they were just hills. Until we passed a high hill where machines were dumping and covering trash and mom said that was the Rumpke dump site and that that big hill of garbage was like the stuff my dad wrote. When we came to a huge cemetery, I could not see fast enough and I closed my eyes for the first time. So much death to record. So much under the ground that I could not remember. So many stones that could no longer be read.

We ascended the fourteen steps to Skyblue's apartment on Riddle Road. I throbbed with anticipation. My temperature was 101.4 and my pulse 126.2. I was geared up, high, like when the waves of drugs sent me spining in my pre-literate anxieties. I'll never forget my first view of Dr. Seiltanzer. He stood at the door, smiling like a frog. Dr. Naval Bombardment introduced me to Skyblue and I was sent to a broken chair and told to sit until summoned. Mary Beth Shut Up For A While sat down on the oak floor by the door with the fifty-four scratches on it across the top. I didn't want to hear what Naval Engagement and P.S. were saying. I didn't want to remember high level scholarship. I closed my eyes and saw the battledore placenta running from my stomach to the ceiling light. A large, dark index finger poked through a crack in the ceiling. It nudged me while I blew bubbles in the blue soup I was swimming in. Voices came to me, saying, "What did you cut this

crap with anyway?" and "You only brought two
bags?" Another foreign voice said, "Lie on your
side, miss. I am always careful." Then the music
started. Gentle waves of sound that I remembered
from my youth, sounds I cannot record. Flutes
twitting. Oboes whining. Trumpets blatting about.
A symphony of gross noise driving me deeper into
the fissure. I thrust my soft head into the darkness,
closed my eyes and listened to the slime bubble past
my ears. A great weight rolled away. A burst of
light. A whop on the back. The battledore tube
thrown away. And Skyblue stood before me, saying, "Would you like a pencil and some paper?"

While Dr. Naval Formation and Mrs. Mary Beth
Dummy went for a walk along Riddle Road, I told
Skyblue my story. I told him about my memory. I
told him the burden of my existence. I told him that
I did not want to go to Kindergarten. That I could
not bear the force of so much data. He told me I
was suffering from catatonic rejectionism. I said that
Dr. Naval Orange had told me that if I don't go
something terrible will happen to me. My dad said
mom would cry and hit the sauce. My dad said he'd
not be able to face his colleagues in Bachelor Hall
if I didn't get a decent education. Skyblue said that
I shouldn't buckle to sentimental fascism. That I
should do what I had to do. He said memory is a
mountain and that I should remember the bear that
went over the mountain and that when he got to the
other side all he saw was the other side of the mountain. When he said, "The transcendental imperatives

of nurturing require solipsistic adumbrations," and "Concentric coincidences in the educational endeavor often mortify the soul" and "Mogigraphia will be the least of the attendant difficulties," I realized he didn't quite understand my problem. I said, "What does all that mean? Can't it be said in simple language?" Skyblue laughed and said, "It means eat shit and go." I realized too that he had been talking to Dr. Naval Exercises and that his advice was not detached from a manifest collegiality. I told Dr. Seiltanzer that I needed advice, that though I knew all things and could speak in multiple tongues, my waning youth had not given me the spiritual fortitude necessary for existential Angst. He promised to write me and help me. I wept for his failure.

Mom and Professor J.D. say I have to start Kindergarten tomorrow. I have read the Revised Code of the State of Ohio and I know if I don't get over to Tomahawk Country Day School by 8:15 tomorrow morning and register for some education I might be taken away and made into into a priest or a football player. That might not be so bad. I could tell the kneeling pubescents all that I'd ever read or heard about God. I could be an assistant coach because I could remember every second of a practice, a game, a chalk-talk, and so they wouldn't need to waste money making films of a game or a practice and I could save them a lot of money and yet not have to suffer so much from remembering all that stuff. I could be a reference library for people interested in Aquinas or Calvin. I could be a fixture in the football hall of fame where I could recite statistics, tell the names of all the visitors, reveal the inventories, repeat all the nasty comments of the players who came to see themselves. There must be some use for me who remembers everything.

(I must say what this is all about.) I fear going to Kindergarten. That's the truth of the matter. The burden of memory will become so great that I wonder if I can endure it. All those kids and all those things being said around me. How will I write fast enough to get it all down? How will I be able to see and listen fast enough to get it all right? I am so frightened that I wrote my first letter six days, four hours, thirty-three minutes and eighteen seconds ago. My pulse was 118.1 and my temperature was 99.9 The letter was to Dr. Skyblue in Cincinnati. I asked him to write me that promised advice and guidance for when I leave my room at home and enter into the classroom. His letter, which I received three minutes and fourteen seconds ago, promised to give me some help. After I read it, my temperature was 98.6 and my pulse 84.2.

Skyblue writes that "Knowledge is better than being informed," that "It is better to be educated than to know things." He says, "Not enough people can't see" and "Too many people are not dumb enough." He writes, "If you hunger and thirst after righteousness, you'll starve to death." "Painting a barn won't make the cows any warmer." "History is the whining of flies." "If you are called to greatness, hang up." "It is better to tell a joke than to be one."

"Cleanliness is next to nothing" and "You rise by gravity and sink by levity." It was the first time I received what is something called wisdom. All these years I've known so much. I've known all I could know. I know all I can know. I can't possibly know more from these five years than I already know. Skyblue's letter was like fresh fish in the market, like live birds on a telephone wire, like snow on the purple crocuses. He is my rock, my mentor. He is my mountain. He says he'll teach me the ways of students and teachers.

He says that I must always have my scripts ready. He says that if someone says to me, "You are a coward," I should say, "I may be a coward but that doesn't prevent me from running when threatened." He says that if someone says, "You should read the Bible," I should answer, "I've already read it and I didn't like the ending." He says that when someone says, "I've forgotten," I should say, "Forgetfulness is the dream of reason. To be able to forget is a blessing of the Almighty. Perfect memory is the death of poetry and the plague of logic." He wrote for my memory, "Memory is a mountain climbed by dwarfs. Remember to forget."

Skyblue says he'll teach more than wisdom. He says he'll teach me how to think and write without metaphor. He'll teach me to simplify my sentences. He'll teach me not to use exclamation points. He'll teach me that syntax is the first principle of order. He'll teach me that denotation is the stuff that dreams are made of. That connotation is the paradise of fools. That style is the absence of connotation. That subordination is not fit to be fed to the hogs. That literary allusion and abstract language are the dandruff of mastodons. That normal word order is golden pears in bowls of silver. That parataxis will make a man out of me. That a comma rightly used is like a drop of rain on a parched eye.

(I think I'm getting everything in order, everything right.) I must travel the dark paths of my third trip into the world, only my third trip since coming home from the womb room, the battledore placenta, the voices from the tube, the finger nudging my watery head, my anterior and posterior fontanels desperately gluing shut while I desperately hoped for pencil, paper and a dictionary. From poetry and wisdom I must go into Kindergarten and I wonder if I can stand it. It sounds like a battledore placenta attached to oblivion. Skyblue says, "It's all right to be afraid. Just don't be a coward." Mary Beth Stupid, Dr. Jonathan David Naval Attache and Dr. Curry have all promised to help me in my adventure into the unknown. They say my teacher will be Miss Muscle Room, who is an expert at sorting crayons, emptying waste baskets and cleaning up vomit. My dad says I should be the Captain Nemo of Tomahawk Country Day School. Mom says, "Do not go gentle into that good night." Dr. Pushta Naguri says, "The lamb lies down with the lion if the lion is dead." The dark night of my youth is over. I go to record the unrecorded babble of my race, shaking like the mountain on which I stand.

At the Rotonde

A GOOD FRENCHMAN thinks of history as a succession of witty sayings. He thinks of the march of events as a sequence of aphorisms, epigrams, *bons mots*. It's speech that makes history. All great events are nothing if something clever can't be said about them. There are no events and there are no great deeds unless they can be smiled away in after-dinner wit. But what if events as experienced are so complicated that they cannot be reduced to a single sentence to accompany a good wine after veal and truffles? What if, like me, you have participated in the grandiose blur of history and you have nothing to say? The answer is very simple; when you have nothing to say you write prose. Another glass of Chateau Droit d' Auteur?

That, Monsieur Gallimard, is why I wrote my prose memoirs. That's why I came from Lausanne to Paris to see you. That's why I asked you to read my manuscript and publish it. Because I lived with the witless Romanovs for twenty years before the revolution. I lived through great historical events. I was inside them. I saw the players. I saw the moves, the panic, the helplessness. I taught them to say in French, "Please pass the butter." I taught Olga, Tatiana, Marie and Anastasia to say in perfect French, "What time is it?" and "Send for the maid." I taught that idiot bleeder the Tsarevich Alexis to say in French, "Bring me my dinner" and "Where is Derevenko?" Derevenko was the sailor who had to follow Alexis everywhere so the last Romanov would not fall down and hemorrhage to death. After dining, when I tried to get them to read Montaigne, Rochefoucauld, La Fontaine, Pascal, Bossuet and Boileau the heirs to an empire tittered and said in perfect French, "Let's play hide-and-seek." They were reeds in a flood. A drowning family does not ask for a sip of wisdom. Waiter, may we have some Brie, please?

French readers will love my memoirs because I was trying to do what Frenchmen have been trying to do since the *Encyclopedia*. I was trying to save a civilization by teaching them French culture. I was trying to bring rationalism to a nation of savage mystics, superstitious fanatics and unreasoning revolutionaries. On board the Standart, the royal yacht, I said to the Tsarevich Alexis, "Tsarevich

Alexis, repeat after me in correct French, please,
'In the misfortune of our best friends, we find something which is not displeasing to us.' " We were
sitting in a lifeboat and rocking quietly in the cold
breeze off the Neva River. Derevenko gave us a
little push ever so often to keep us going. Just as
the Tsarevich began the sentence, I noticed that the
Emperor Nicholas II in his trolley car conductor's
uniform was looking down over us. He smiled his
heavy German smile and said in French — none of
them could speak Russian well —, "The Tsarevich is
tired now. Let him rest. We leave tomorrow for
Livadia. He can study his French there. Monsieur
Gilliard, you should prepare to accompany us on the
royal train." Derevenko gave us a big shove; we
rocked in our lifeboat shelter. The Tsarevich lay
down in the bottom of the boat and giggled. Removing my straw boater and putting my pince-nez into
my coat pocket, I looked across the river to the
golden spire on the cathedral in the Peter and Paul
Fortress where the revolutionaries had died in the
Alexis ravelin. I realized that history is an inventory
of prisons. Destiny is formed in the pamphlets of
the anarchists. This Chateau Droit d'Auteur is ex-
cellent, I must say. I congratulate you, Monsieur
Gallimard, for selecting it. The Russians have no
good wines.

Such lovely places the Romanovs lived in; Tsar-
skoe Selo, Peterhof, Spala, the Standart, the Winter
Palace, the summer retreat at Livadia overlooking the
Black Sea. By the lovely Yalta and the blood-drench-

ed Sevastopol. Where we went that last summer of 1914 before the flood. We boarded the lovely royal blue railroad cars for what we did not know then was the last journey to that paradise. I traveled in the first train that carried supplies, guards, servants, the train that went first in case bombs had been planted on the tracks. At least Rasputin wasn't along; otherwise I might have hoped for a detonation. I would gladly have risked an explosion if it might take him with it. A filthy, stinking man. A holy man, a starets, who had walked to Mt. Athos and to Jerusalem. Rasputin, "the dissolute one," who was the spiritual advisor to the Empress Alexandra. Rasputin from Tobolsk, where he left a wife and children. Rasputin seeming to heal the bleeding Tsarevich. Rasputin, who scratched the lice in his crotch in the presence of the Empress and fingered Anastasia. He should have healed Queen Victoria, the cause of all that hemophilia. That fat British foo-foo who fouled the blood of the royal families of Europe. The Empress the granddaughter of Queen Victoria, who was not around to see the disaster she caused. Rasputin speaking his peasant's Russian to the Empress of All the Russias, who spoke French, English and German. Your French readers will appreciate the irony of the fact that he was from Tobolsk; that's where the Romanovs were first taken when they were arrested after the revolution. The last photograph of them shows them sunning themselves on a roof. Religious people have no use for irony. The Brie has started to run at the center. Try a bite.

When we arrived at Livadia in the summer of 1914, we sat on the stone balcony overlooking the Black Sea and read *Les Miserables*. Olga, Tatiana and Marie in their pinafores, bad breath and clinking minds. Posing in their polka dot dresses, front and back. The Tsarevich playing with boys recruited to be his playmates. The boys drilled by Derevenko and pulled about in a wagon by the sailor Nagorny. As if the Tsarevich could ever be strong enough or live long enough to be a soldier. Pulled and drilled by those same sailors who after the revolution refused to have anything to do with the royal family. It never occurred to the royalty that those mustached sailors might not like the Romanovs, that they might have desires the royal family could not conceive of.

The Emperor and Autocrat of All the Russias shouldn't have been surprised that his virgin daughters flirted with and fondled the soldiers of the revolution in Tobolsk. The only men they could get close enough to touch were sailors, soldiers and their Communist guards. Until they were shot in Ekaterinburg and their bodies soaked with oil and burned. I wasn't surprised because Olga, Tatiana and Marie asked me questions in perfect French, questions which cannot be answered in the French of the academies. Anastasia didn't understand what was going on. But the older daughters knew something was happening to them and they asked questions which could be answered only in a bed. Where no language is necessary. Language is a system of words which are supposed to define our feelings but never can except by indirection. History is a glance off to the side. Destiny is forged by offhand remarks. Our fate is set by the incorrect words we choose. In Russia I drank mostly Italian and German wines, but they weren't nearly as good as this Chateau Droit d'-Auteur. Finish the bottle.

That last summer at Livadia, just before the world exploded, Olga, the oldest daughter, mind you nineteen, asked me to get her a copy of *Madame Bovary*. I said, "Mademoiselle Olga Nickolaevna, that book is not on the approved list. It is not a book for young ladies." "Get it," she said. I rolled my eyes up, shrugged my shoulders, held my palms up and went into my room and brought her my copy. She promised not to tell. Olga read it that night. The next day she asked me to explain to her what was going on between Emma Bovary and Rodolphe and between Madame Bovary and Leon. I blushed and said that they were having love affairs. She said, "What do people do when they have love affairs?" The tongue of a teacher should never wag. I felt myself slipping into the Black Sea. I told her to ask Miss Orchard, the governess. She said, "What do you and Miss Orchard do in your room at night? What is all that noise?" Aristocrats are unfit to govern because they don't tell their children the truth. Democracy is the government for lovers. Don't you think that's interesting? I mean Olga and her questions. Your readers will love it as much as I love this wine and this Brie.

Tatiana. What can I say. She had the skin of a Faberge egg. She looked as if she were always surprised by a mushroom, quartz, butterflies, snow. So lovely her folded flesh. Nubile at thirteen. Dead at twenty-one. She played the piano with the skill of a polar bear, but she was the most skilled of the lot. She ordered the others around and caressed her mother. She told me one time, "Monsieur Gilliard, I want to marry a peasant. Can you arrange it?" When I replied that that was quite impossible she pinched my rump. Did that really happen or is my mind distorted by all the snowballs they threw at me at Tsarskoe Selo? Did Tatiana Nickolaevna really whisper to me that my tongue reminded her of something she saw once in a dream or has my brain been blasted by the thought of all that royal virginity blown away in a basement? When I asked her what she saw in her dream she used a French word I'm sure she learned from the sailors on the Standart. I see even now her gray eyes and auburn hair as she whispered in my ear where we sat on the balcony overlooking the Black Sea, overlooking the Crimean mountains and firs, overlooking the fields where so many Russians died in the Crimean War, "What is that bulge in your pocket?" A proposal is the right choice of words. Indirection is the invitation of the innocent. The right word leads to indecent thought. I was wrong; the Crimean wines were good. Maybe even better than what we're drinking.

Marie was the one who would have passed on the bad heredity, that English blight that cost me my job. Marie talked about children and marriage. She wanted it. She wanted to dive into a royal bed and watch her belly swell. Her children were the bullets of the revolution. Those lead babies born in a split second. Passing through her womb in record time and became her progeny. Covered with blood so that the royal bleeding might end. She carried the family line to its logical conclusion. Bad blood creates bad blood. When I was separated from the family in Ekaterinburg, as I watched them get into a carriage, it was Marie who turned in the mist and waved to me. It was she who stepped last into the carriage that would carry them out of my sight forever. Motherhood is an accident of history. Generations are the revenge of nobility. And isn't it true that if there were truth in wine we could say what we think? If there were truth in wine we could see that history is the deceit of syntax. What metaphors we must make, Monsieur Gallimard, what metaphors.

Then there was dear little Anastasia, shot just as she was coming into her own. Her pretty little blood spattered onto the wall of that cellar so that the soldiers of the White Army could dig out the slugs for souvenirs. I can imagine her standing there with her hands crossed over her navel, trying to keep the bullets from hitting her future. I wonder what color the slugs were when they emerged from her royal back. I wonder what color the slugs took on as they passed through her skin, her viscera, her hemophiliac ovaries. I wonder how quickly the bleeding soaked into her cute little white dress. I wonder if she had time enough to cross herself before her fingers spun up into the beams. I wonder how she smelled as her oil-soaked corpse sizzled in the Urals. The aristocracy are sheep. Royalty breeds itself into oblivion. More wine?

One night at Lavadia, there was a knock on my door. A timid knock, not like the knocks of Miss Orchard when she came in for a mug of tea and what she called "a little praise God for His blessings." There that little girl stood like a Faberge egg, one of those diamond and amethyst encrusted golden eggs given as gifts on Easters, one of those royal eggs that had a button that could be pressed and a bird would come out the top, flutter its wings and pop back down into that shell of jewels and gold. "Oh my dear," I said, "whatever are you doing here at this hour?" She said, in her Romanov twitter, "Monsieur Gilliard, Miss Orchard is snoring so loudly that I can't sleep. May I spend the night with you?" Me, a Frenchman, and she asks a question like that. When Miss Orchard discovered us in the morning, it was the end of mugs of tea and "a spot of all right." If you sip at the cup of iniquity, innocence is the spice of life. Fill my glass. When opportunity knocks, unbutton your trousers. I know your readers will like my book.

After Ekaterinburg, my three years of investigations in siberia did no good. When the White Army arrived, we found the contents of the Tsarevich's pockets, royal belt buckles and a well manicured finger from the Empress. So I escaped through

Japan and the United States, back to my studies begun twenty years before in Switzerland and then to Lausanne and the Legion of Honor. Now no one listens to my lectures, my memoirs, my aphorisms, my epigrams, my *bons mots*. Surely one who experienced it is best able to tell what it all was. French culture failed to save an empire. It's a good story. I remember once the train stopped on the way to Livadia. It was terribly hot and we stopped by a river to cool ourselves. The girls dared me to race them down a high hill of sand. I ran and fell and rolled into the water. They screamed and laughed as they slid by on silver platters. I was wrong; the Crimean wines were better than this cheap French swill. Would you be so kind, Monsieur Gallimard, as to pay for the meal? You see, the Communists took all my money when I fled the country. They said, as they counted it, "Anyone who speaks French is an enemy of the people."

Night Flight to Stockholm

OWE ALL THIS to Gabriel Ratchet. It was he who arranged for the round-trip ticket, two seats side by side, on Scandinavian Airlines, got me my reservation in the King Gustaf Holiday Inn, deodorized my basket, put in the new sheets, put on my new, formal black sack with the white ribbon drawstring around the top and bathed my suppurating stumps for the journey. He even carried one end of my wicker laundry basket when I went aboard. In the darkness, I heard him instructing the stewardesses as to how to clean me, how to feed and water me and when to turn me. I heard money changing hands. I heard his stomachy laugh and the ladies' bovine grunts. I think I heard a

stewardess pat his little bald head. Then came my first lift-off. The great surge of the old Boeing 747 sliding my butt and stumps against one end of the basket and then the floating and my ears popping. Into glorious, golden dreams in my black chute. Into non-stop gliding through images of published books, careful emendations, green surgical gowns, the rustle of paper money, the clink of prizes and the odor of immortality. It was Gabriel Ratchet who gave me this slow drifting in the darkness 50,00 feet over Iceland, the North Atlantic, Ireland, England, the North Sea and Norway as we, as I hear from the pilot, descend into our landing pattern for Stockholm and me about to meet the king of Sweden and, I assume, his wife and all the little royalties. I wonder what they'll sound like; I wonder how they'll smell.

I owe all this to Gabriel because he is an expert in contracts. He's made contracts for musicians, painters, sculptors, quarterbacks, pole vaulters, jugglers, born-again Christians and presidents. He's negotiated the careers of farmers, professors, poets, priests, baseball pitchers, terrorists and airline pilots. For the past thirty years he's had his hand in more success than you can shake a scalpel at because of his immense number of contacts. He says he brought it with him from the womb. I can believe it. Gabriel — his clients call him Gabe or Gabby — was born on the western slope of Muckish Mountain in Donegal in 1935, exact day unknown he says, when his mother saw some white horses hung with silver bells. He came to Chicago, IL., he says, when the potato crop failed around Bloody Foreland in 1951. I don't remember any potato famines in Ireland since the nineteenth century, but I'm always willing to lend him an ear and listen to his stories. He came to Chicago, he says, because he is a creature of our own flesh and blood and likes a city where every man has his price. He says his contracting business didn't go well at first. In fact, he was on his last leg when he met Isobel Gowdie in October, 1956, in the Chicago Art Institute while he and she were standing and staring at some water lilies by Monet. According to his own account, Gabriel sighed and said, "Hell, Peg Powler can paint better than that." Isobel, having an eye to the main chance, imme- diately answered, "Richard Tarlton has one foot in the grave. Can you give him a hand?" Gabe's life as a public servant and a successful entrepreneur began with that moment because he negotiated a contract whereby for a shake and a cut Ambroise Pare became the first wealthy one-armed undertaker in Hellwaine, ME.

I first met Gabe in the lobby of the Palmer House in December of 1977 when I was there for an MLA convention. He was loitering around the packed lobby, looking, I later found out, for failures with whom he could do some business. He was sidling about, handing out, quietly and covertly, little business cards, red letters on green, that gave his name, Gabriel "Ballybofey" Ratchet, his office, 1313 Spoorne Ave., Chicago, his telephone number, 393- 6996, his office hours, "At Your Convenience," his profession, "Contractor," and his motto, "Don't limp in obscurity; get a leg up on this world." He gave me his last card and said he'd never seen so many potential clients. He said he'd had his eye on me for some time and I was cut to the quick. We chatted, there in that mob, for a while and I asked him about himself. He told me that he was so short because of that potato famine in his youth. His nose and ears were gnarled because his mother had been frightened by Peg O'Nell when she, his dear mother, was nursing him and her left teat had immediately dried up while in his mouth. His teeth were rotted out and his head bald because his wife of two years, Joan Tyrrie of Creke Abbey, MT., had tried to poison him with bat slobber. He managed, he said, to overcome the poison by eating stuffed grasshoppers, roasted ants and mice roasted whole and threw her into the Chicago River. He said she'd been bad from the start and he was surpised his marriage in the year of 1955 lasted the two years that it did. Gabe said that her stepmother had given her a bottle of flat beer and some sour bread for a dowry and that after their marriage in Calkett Hall all she wanted to do was to be friendly with the goats and comb their beards. He said there was saltpeter in her heaven and gold in her hell and that her angels were sufficiently embodied to be impeded by their armor and damaged by gunpowder. I told him my problems and he said that I was too old to fool around any longer, that I would have to fight tooth and nail to make it. I said I'd call him if I needed his service.

I needed his help a lot sooner than I thought then because my paper which I presented at that MLA convention was laughed to scorn. When I began my opening remarks I heard tittering. When I asked for silence, they guffawed. When I introduced my paper — "Metaphorical Thinking as the Cause of the Collapse of British and American Literature" by Professor Meyric Casaubon, Department of English, University of Tylwyth Teg, Wales, OR. — they hooted and snarled and shot out their lips. They waggled their beards and gnashed their teeth on their pipe stems. Even my old friend, Bock Urisk, who claimed he could hear grass growing, could run so fast when he was young that he had to keep one leg over his shoulder to stay in sight, could break stones on his thighs they were so hard and could spin a windmill by blowing through one nostril, waved his open palms past his ears and held his nose. I got the message when Richard Tynney of Gorleston, DE., the chairman of the panel, and Sir John Shepe of Wanstrowe, IA., the moderator, got up, dropped their pants and showed me their bare asses. I was mooned for metaphors and that was the end, I thought. I walked off the stage, my green suit striking among the black turtle necks, my thick black hair bobbing over the seated howlers, my hooked nose, my protuberant chin and my green eyes lifted high in disdain, even though I was without skin and my huge belly bounced and rumbled. I walked out of the room, my white Converse All-Stars squeaking on the waxed floors, my white tie and my blue shirt spotted with my sweat. I sneaked to my room, took off my Phi Beta Kappa pin and threw it into the toilet. I decided then to go back to what I'd always been doing anyway, writing fiction. I took out the green card with the red letters.

It was a Thursday when I lifted the phone and called him. I said, "Gabe, I'm going to be sixty-six tomorrow, Friday, January 13, 1978, and I've been writing fiction all my life and no one's ever published a word of it and I'd give my left pinkie to get into *Paris Review*." And I did because Gabriel was interested at once and told me that he'd get in touch with me the next day because he thought he might find a buyer. He did. The next day Gabe came around and said he had a friend, Tom Reid, whose ancestor was killed at the battle of Pinkie in 1547 and who needed to get his self-respect back. According to Gabriel, Tom had agreed to see to it that my story, "Livid With Age," would be published in *Paris Review* for my left pinkie. And he did. He told me to type my story, double-spaced, on clean white paper. Not to use eraseable paper. He said I should make my setting exact in place and time, not to moralize at the end of the story and to get rid of the false intensifiers like "literally," "really," "utterly," "just," "veritable," "absolutely," "very" and "basically." Create emphasis by syntax, he said. He also told me to clean the sweat stains off. I did all that and when my story came out, I went to Dr. Dodypol and had the finger removed surgically and under anasthesia. His head nurse, Kate Crackernuts,

wrapped the finger in cotton bandages and in red
tissue paper with a yellow ribbon around it and I
walked out a published author and weighing three
ounces less than when I walked in. And made
money on it too, because the operation cost fifty
dollars and I was paid sixty for my story.

A month after the appearance of "Livid With
Age," I sent another story out, "Liam Sexob Lives in
Loveland," to *TriQuarterly*. It seemed like it came
back the same day, although of course it didn't, and
I knew that I needed Gabriel Ratchet again and his
influence. I found him sitting in the Trywtyn Tratyn
Pub, drinking Habitrot and flirting with Jenny
Greenteeth. "Look, Gabe," I said, "I need help. I'd
give my left testicle to get my story in *TriQuarterly*."
Gabe didn't even look at me when he said, "Make it
two and I think I can get you a deal." I allowed as to
how I'd probably go along with it and he said he'd
talk to Marmaduke Langdale, who needed them for
his Whitsun Rejoicings. Gabe did and I did. Dr.
Nepier from Lydford in Bercks and his head nurse,
Sarah Skelbourn, removed them on a cold Friday in
December of 1978. Sarah wrapped them in white
bandages, green tissue paper and red ribbons. I took
them to Gabriel, who was satisfied with the mer-
chandise and told me that Marmaduke Langdale said
I should change the title of the story to "Silence on
the Rive Gauche," change the name of the main
character Liam Sexob to Burd Isobel, eliminate the
doublings, get rid of the colloquial style, erase the
tear stains from the margins of pages 4, 14 and 22,

and stop using exclamation points, dashes, under-
linings for emphasis and the series of periods that
indicate ellipses. I did all that. Retyped the story on
good, twenty pound linen bond and sent it off to
TriQuarterly. They accepted it within a week and I
was on my way to my second story in print.

When "Silence on the Rive Gauche" came out, I
asked Gabriel Ratchet to be my permanent agent.
He agreed and in July of 1979 Dr. Louis Marie Sini-
strari and his colleague, Isidore Liseaux, removed
my left hand which I figured I didn't need anyway
because I can only type with my right hand and
right arm, wrapped it in blue and red striped gift
paper, tied it with black ribon, and sent it to Mr.
Greatorex, the Irish Stroker, who wrote back from
the Island of Hy Brasil, MD., that I should stop using
participial phrases, get the inactive detail out of my
descriptions, stop using literary language with its
euphemisms and circumlocutions and not use ex-
clamations such as "needless to say," "to my amaze-
ment" and "I don't have to tell you." He also suggested that I not send in pages with blood stains on
them. I did everything he said and *Esquire* accepted
my story, "Moles' Brains and the Right to Life."

Even though I was still anemic from my last publication, I decided in January of 1980 to bid for the
New Yorker. Gabe sent out the message and Durant
Hotham wrote from Yatton Keynel, ME., that he
would do it for a pair of ears if I would promise to
stop using abnormal word order, get rid of the *faux-
naif* narrator, eliminate all cliches from my narrative,

would isolate point of view in one character or one narrator and would clean my snot off the manuscript. I did what he said and sent in the manuscript of "Muckelawee." Durant wrote back his thanks for the contract and told me to visit Peg Powler at 1369 Kelpie Street and she would have some directions for me. I went. She had directions and told me to go to Dr. Arviragus at the Abbey Lubbers Clinic. I went. When I walked out of the Clinic, I had my ears in a red and gold bag tied at the top with a green ribbon. The stumps on the sides of my head tingled in the cold air as I walked out into a new reputation as one of the finest stort story writers in America.

When I suggested a book of short stories to Gabriel, he shivered. He suggested that I rest for a while and get myself together before I made any more deals. I told him he'd made a lot of money off my publications and that he would make a lot more. Just to do his work as my agent and let me worry about the parts. He did admit that he had an offer. That he needed a left arm, even if there was no hand attached to it. A Dr. William Drage of Hitchin, AR., needed it to fit out Margaret Barrance so that she could attend a ball because not having a left arm there was nothing for her to lay across the shoulder of her male partner while she danced. Gabriel told me that I would have to go to Hitchin for the transplant. I agreed and I did in March of 1981. But before he removed the left arm, he told me that the deal was contingent on my editing my manuscript carefully, to carefully control the secondary patterns, to make the deuteragonist more important in all the stories, to research materials for the stories, to make the stories more weird, more strange, more uncomfortable for the reader. Clean the ear wax off my pages. I promised I'd do all he told me to do and he took my arm and sewed it onto Margaret, who six months later danced in her first ball at the age of thirty-three, wearing a blue and gold dress with a red sash around the waist, while Doubleday published my collection of short stories, *The Cry of Horse and Hattock* (September, 1981).

Because my recovery times were lengthening, I decided that a novel should be my next reduction and when I mentioned it to Gabriel Ratchet he fell on the floor and chortled. I told him to get his little carcass off the floor and get to work. He did. He got bids for my nose, my feet, my legs, my eyes, my penis and my kidneys. I bid one left foot. The law firm of Morgue, Arsile and Maglore handled the negotiations and in February of 1982 Ratchet finalized the contract with Miss Ruth Tongue of Somerset, KS., by which I agreed to furnish her with one left foot in return for the publication of my novel, *Flibberty Gibbet*, by Knopf. My part of the contract was that I had to stop misusing "transpire," "problematical," "livid," "momentarily," "presently" and "loin." My sentences were to be made more simple. I was to use more active verbs with agents doing actions. I was to get out the melodrama. I also agreed not to use any anthropomorphizing metaphors, not to personify anything not human, to make only direct descriptions of characters, objects and actions and not to leak urine on my manuscript. Gabriel also negotiated an interesting addendum to the contract and that was that if the book could be made to win a national prize then my part of the bargain was the left foot and whole left leg. Wouldn't you know; Ms. Tongue got the whole leg when *Flibberty Gibbet,* clad in a dust jacket of red, black and orange, won the National Book Award for 1982. They carried me up to the podium in a rocking chair and I shook hands for the last time when I accepted the award.

Rachet's account books, which he read to me before I left O'Hare, read as follows after that:

April 4, 1983: Right foot. To Tommy Rawhead of Asmoday, ND. Complicate the emotional and psychological dimensions of the action. Careful selection of names. Vary sentence rhythms. Tonal variation. Shit off pages. Novel: *Brachiano's Ghost.* Macmillan. Black and grey cover. Red chapter headings. Plus right leg: Pulitzer Prize. Done.

July 16, 1984: Right hand. To Elaby Gathen of Hackpen, MI. Correct spelling of "existence," "separate" and "pursue." No redundancy in nouns and verbs and their modifiers. Play games with readers. No slobbering on pages. Book of short stories: *The Blue Hag of Winter.* Random House. Gold on black cover. Red title pages. Right arm also: O'Henry Award, St. Lawrence Award for Fiction and Chair at Columbia. Done.

February 10, 1985: Two eyes. To Billy Blind of Systern, DE. No use of "etc.," the suffix "-wise," correct use of "as." No rhetorical questions in narrative. No openings with dialogue. No flashbacks. Include all senses in descriptions. No pus on pages. Two volume novel: *Sammael.* Little, Brown. Red, green and blue cover. Nobel Prize. Done.

As I float over the shadowed northern world, I think now that we all go off into darknesses, bit by bit, piece by piece, part by part. We all disintegrate into our words, our sentences, our paragraphs, our narratives. We scatter our lives into photographs, letters, certificates, books, prizes, lies. We ride out the light until the records break one by one. We sit out the days until the suns get dimmer and dimmer. We lie about in the gathering shadows until North America, South America, Australia, Antarctica, Asia, Africa and Europe lie about on the dark waters of our globe. It is crack time in the world of flesh. It is shatter time in the world of limbs. It is splatter time in the world of bones. It is the last splinter of the word. I have tasted the double-deal. I have smelled the sleight-of-hand. I have heard the cryptic whisper. I have felt the cold riddle. Because no one stands apart from his stone. No one laughs apart from his crust. No one breathes apart from his shriveling. No one speaks apart from his silence. To lie down in a wicker basket is not to lie apart. To be turned on soft, pus-soaked sheets is not to be turned alone. To be fed through tubes is not to eat alone. To drink and choke is to spit up for all. To float through the night is the journey we all take sooner or later until the bright and shining morning star breaks and there is no more.

I can feel the huge plane starting to descend. My seventy-four year old ears are popping. The stewardess who smells like a dead dog has already rolled me over so that I won't aspirate if I vomit. She's strapped me tightly in place on my two seats. I can feel the safety belts across my guts and chest. I feel the descent into darkness and I know that I have not given up anything that I could not do without. I know that you can live with less than you came in with. I know that wholeness is not everything and that if you will give an eye for a prize you'll be a sure winner. I can feel my long, white hair sliding and shaking over my stumpy ears as the plane bucks and banks for the landing. I can imagine the attendants in black knickers with the little black bows by the knees who will carry me onto the clapping stage. I can imagine the old black king squinting through his thick glasses down into the wicker basket with the two handles and the white Cannon sheets. As my snot begins to leak out over my upper lip, I can hear myself asking him to clean the ear wax out of my shallow ears so that I can hear him clearly when he extols the virtues of long-suffering, when he prattles about how some people overcome severe handicaps and go on to greatness, when he maunders about the indomitable will of the human spirit, while the old black queen gurgles and snickers down at the heady, winning lump. And I hope it's a prince, princess or princeling who will hold the microphone down into the basket so that while pus oozes from my eye sockets I can whisper my acceptance speech. I hope I can control my saliva. I hope I don't shed tears. And finally there will be the flowers to add their smells to the noises, the tastes and the temperatures. I wonder if anyone will manage to get a sip of Champagne to me. That thumping, bumping and bouncing must be the runway.

Night Flight to Miami

I MADE THE arrangements. It took me a year from last March when I flew out of Havana to Miami, a flight on Newfoundland Airways, Inc. Landing in Miami at 2:30 A.M., I had to sit in the airport until 9:30 that morning for my flight out to Wichita, Kansas. While I waited, I ate composted liver and onions from a steam table, I read cretin-created stories in the *Atlantic* and shopped through souvenirs that should be forgotten. There was a language being spoken around me that I didn't understand. It could have been Bulgarian, Polish or Rumanian, for all I knew. Janitors pushed electric vacuum cleaners around on the carpets and left

more dirt than they picked up. The overhead speakers
crackled now and then but no one could understand what they said. The air conditioning turned
the tasteless building into an arctic waste.

Now it's March again, my companero is supposed
to be here and I'm sitting in the Miami Airport
again. It's 4:30 in the morning. The liver and onions
taste the same, the magazine stories are still awful,
I don't understand the overhead speakers and I'm
shivering. I'm waiting for Lobo and his three musicians, the Havana Hotshots, to arrive — if they do.
Because who knows what's going on. They were
supposed to leave Havana three days ago at 1:30 in
the morning. They still have not arrived. Who knows
where their plane is. It could be out there right
now, it could be floating in the Gulf Stream, it
could be landing in Moscow or Czechoslovakia, it
could be changing a tire in Angola, it could be
seized by the blockade of the North Americans.
The pilot could be asleep and the automatic pilot
could be taking them to the great socialist paradise
after death. Whatever is going on, I know the Havana Hotshots are singing too loudly; I know that
Lobo is trying to remember who is meeting him in
Miami and I know that I must wait until they arrive
because the arrangements have been made. How will
I know when he arrives? How will he know that he
is here?

The problem begins with the fact that my friend
Lobo is from the province of Camaguey in Cuba.
His real name is not Lobo because in Camaguey no

one is given a name and so the people can't remember what each is called. They don't care. Lobo thinks he might be named after a fudge with macadamia nuts that is imported from Spain, he might be named after a beer served at the Floridita or he might be named for his lupine characteristics. But they don't import fudge into Camaguey, there is no beer there and certainly there are no wolves there. There never were any wolves in Camaguey — if that's in fact where Lobo is from.

Lobo says that no one knows what to call the people from Camaguey. It's a problem they don't know exists, and, besides, he always says, "Companero, Camaguey is no paradise." It has been suggested that the people be called "Camaguitos," "Camaguinis" or "Camaguacitos." I suggested once that they be called "Camaguanos" but Lobo said that no one would ever be able to spell or remember that name. I told him that the people ought to call their baseball team the "Guanos" because of the bats in Camaguey. But there are no bats in Camaguey, nor is there any sense of humor. Lobo did remark that he often wondered why the people never cheered for their team. He supposed they couldn't cheer without a name for their team. They would forget it anyway. I asked him when he last saw a baseball game. He couldn't remember because their team never plays at home.

The reason, I found out, that they never play at home is that no one quite knows where Camaguey is. It's not in the west; it's not in the east. It's not in the central part of Cuba. It's somewhere between central Cuba and eastern Cuba, which, Lobo observed, makes it hard to find. No one knows how to give directions to it. If you travel east from Havana to go to the province of Guantanamo, you go through Camaguey. But most people go around it because they don't know where through begins. Airline pilots trying to fly there usually end up in Granma or Tunas. When they land in those provinces beyond Camaguey, the passengers get off and say, "This isn't Camaguey. Where is it?" And the natives all point up with their middle fingers.

Once the great reporter from *The Cincinnati Post*, Lew Smith, came to Havana to do a story on Camaguey. I introduced him to my friend Lobo, who promised to help. Lew asked how he could get to the province. Lobo said, "You can fly there." I said, "But how can a pilot find it if no one knows where it is?" Lew looked disturbed, popped another Mojito down, and asked, "You mean pilots set out for Camaguey even though they don't know where it is?" "Of course," said Lobo, "why do you think the people built the airport? Besides, the pilots know where it is. They just can't find it." Lew smiled his crooked smile and said, "How do I meet the pilot?" Lobo said, "It can be arranged. I will arrange it." The crafty Lew said, "How will I know when I'm there?" Lobo said, "I will be there to meet you. So will all the people. They will clap and cheer as you descend from the plane. The noise will wake up the sleeping pilot. They will welcome you to Camaguey but they won't remember your name. They will cut sugar cane, if there is any, and they will erect a monument to celebrate your visit, if there is any cement or stone. They will say, 'Who is this guy, anyway?' "

Lew pondered the situation. "But," he said, "how will I know what to write? What will I put in my column?" "Oh ho," Lobo said, "what difference does it make? Everything about Camaguey is true. Say that it is no paradise and that the people have many problems but they are working hard to overcome them even though they forget from day to day what they are. Say that the people are happy and that they welcome whoever he is from whatever newspaper in whatever place he comes from. They will say, 'What's his name?' and start the monument.

"Above all, " Lobo said, "you can write how they sing to you because all the great singers in Cuba come from Camaguey. There they have the Desi Arnaz Institute of Song — you will be taken on a tour of it — where three young men at a time are given guitars and maracas. They sing in three's because the Camaguanos can't count past three. They get confused, forget the next number, lose track of the people, and they don't care anyway. The three young men are told to go to the Zapata Swamp in the province of Cienfuegos and learn music. They do — for five years. When they return, they all sound alike. They try to learn how to tune their instruments so they can sing the songs they learn by imitating the sounds of the mosquitos, the turkey vultures and the crocodiles. No one undersands the words of the songs. Neither do the singers. The words of the songs change from one singing to another because the singers forget the words."

Lobo says that his job is to make arrangements for the musicians to sing in Havana. He contacts bars, clubs and hotels and arranges for the musicians to sing while the tourists are enjoying themselves. When I asked him how he contacted the musicians in Camaguey, he said he telephoned them but he didn't remember the number. He puts in a call, the musicians go to the airport and fly to Havana and he meets them. Lobo admits that they usually ask first to meet the reporter who once came to their province and whose monument is made of guitars and maracas smashed and shattered by North American tourists. Lobo takes the singers to the Riviera Hotel, the Deauville Hotel, the Floridita Bar, anywhere and everywhere, and pushes them through the door so that whenever the tourists order a meal or a drink the musicians can sing as loudly as they can. This causes the tourists to say, "Oh wow. Isn't this great? Real Cuban music." Lobo says, "It's not Cuban music. It's Camaguano music."

When I asked Lobo if he made his living by arranging for the singers, he said he didn't know. He said he was paid 320 pesos a month for his work. When I observed that he never seemed to have anything to do except talk to me, he said he didn't. He said the musicians go to whichever hotel or bar they feel like going to or whichever bar or hotel they happen to be in front of and go in and play. He said that everything is owned by the state and, therefore, they could go in and play and no one could say anything. They are part owners of the place. Lobo said he was active in being the Director of Foreign Relations for Cuban Music and said that he hoped that reporter who went to Camaguey would return and put the musicians in his paper. He said it would make them famous, help tourism and maybe make it possible for the musicians to go to North America.

He talked of sending the musicians to other socialist countries in order for them to participate in internationalism. I said, "Where would you like to send your musicians first?" He answered, "Miami." I told him that Miami is not in or part of a socialist country. "Oh companero," he answered, "it's part of Camaguey. Miami is filled with Camaguanos. That reporter from North America said so." "Lew Smith," I said. "Whatever his name," Lobo said. "Thousands of people have left our province to live in Miami even though it's no paradise and has many problems to solve. We consider it part of our province. I understand it's just like Camaguey. I woud like to see it with my musicians." "Well," I said, "when you arrive I'll be there to meet you if the pilot can find it and doesn't land in Lake Okeechobee. But I won't remember your name and we'll raise a monument to you. The monument will be made from White Castle hamburger wrappers and soft drink cups from McDonald's." "I don't understand," said Lobo. "What are these things you talk about?" I looked at him and said, "I don't remember. No one cares anyway."

Lobo asked if he could see a baseball game when he came to Miami. I told him I only went to night games and he said, "Why only night games?" And I said, "Because there aren't any lights." Lobo tried to think about that for a while and then said, "Do they play baseball where you come from?" "Sure," I said, "I'm from Kansas and it's kind of like Camaguey. It's located between other things and no one knows quite where it is. If you go there it's hard to know when you arrive. No one quite knows where the borders are. Airline pilots trying to find it land in Colorado or California." Lobo asked, "What's the music like there?" "We have the Ralph Stanley Institute of Song. If you go there you can get a guided tour. When certain young men turn sixteen, we select five of them because we can't count further than that. We give one a mandolin, one a guitar, one a banjo, one a fiddle and one a double bass. We send them out behind a barn and tell them to learn to play. After five years they usually are still trying to tune their instruments." "Blessed Granma," said Lobo, "can they play any place they want to?" "No," I said, "our province is a capitalist province. The musicians must make a contract and be paid for their work." "Do they make a living?" "No." "How do they live? " "They don't," I said.

Lobo thought about this for a while and said, "What is your name?" "Why, it's Skyblue," I said. "Skyblue?" he said. "Yes, indeed," I said, "I've told you that a hundred times." "Why are you called that?" "I don't know. In Kansas people are very careful about naming people so it could be that I'm called that because of the color of my eyes, because I was a little bundle of joy from heaven or because they just forgot my real name. In Kansas the people say, 'Out of sight; out of mind.' Because of the dust, most things are out of sight and therefore out of mind. They forget too. I tell you what. I'll call you 'Lobo' and you call me 'Skyblue.' You think you can remember that?" Lobo smiled and said, "Companero Skyblue, do you think you'll ever bring your music into Camaguey?" "No way," I said, "if you promise to keep your Camaguanos out of Kansas." "It's a deal," he said. I patted him on the shoulder and said, "Let's go have a drink somewhere. Let's go worship the great god Mojito." "Yes," he said, "I remember Mojito. Once in Camaguey we made a statue of him with potato peels." "And Lobo," I said, "could we go somewhere where we could have our drink in quiet, where there are no musicians?"

"It can be arranged," he said. "I will take care of it."

Y MOTHER DIED — I think of terminal sexual climax — on November 5, 1971, while watching goo-goo eyed King Kong finger Fay Wray in his king-sized palm, and I inherited $200,000. King Kong was rolling his watery eyes around, trying to focus on that little white fetus in his left hand, lowering his submarine-sized, black, greasy right index finger toward screaming Fay, mom was squirming in her seat, the people behind me were yelling "Down in front" because I'm so tall and always had to sit downfront with mom, who was eating hot, buttered popcorn and drinking Diet Pepsi. A man behind me was tapping me on the shoulder and saying, "Hey buddy, we'd like to see

the film too so how about scooting down in your
seat a little" when mom dropped her popcorn and
her Diet Pepsi, stood up, grabbed her breasts and
fell, twitched, tried to crawl under the seats but
couldn't because she got stuck on the wet gum
stuck under the seats and because we were strapped
together. She pulled me over a little when the strap
pulled tight and the guy behind me said "Thanks"
and I watched the show until she stopped twitching.
Six months later I got the money and that's how I
got my own movie house, the Omega I. I thought,
and still do, that it was a fitting way to use those
"pennies from heaven," or should I say "dollars
from heaven," because she died right here, left aisle,
center section, row four, seat eight. That seat she
died in is now up in the projection booth — not
"projection room," as some call it — and bolted to
the floor, just as it was in the auditorium, so that I
can sit straight up while the movie projectors are
clicking gaily along through "Silent Running," "Leo
the Last," "Clockwork Orange" or "The Tenth Vic-
tim." The light flickering out over the seats and
through the motes of dust. The nitrogen-filled tung-
sten lamp glowing. The sprockets slipping those
frames through, twenty-four per second, the shutters wheeling, the Maltese cross spinning left, the
film flicking past the lens and through the light,
sliding smoothly through the soundhead, and me
sitting on mom's death seat and watching out one of
the camera ports, looking down on my movie house,
looking down at the four or five people who have

paid ($1.00) their way in because there's nothing else to do in their dying neighborhood, a neighborhood, Spitzer's Corner, made up mainly of asphalt-covered parking lots, empty lots where urban renewal has knocked down the old houses and replaced them with wrecked cars on cinder blocks, and one main road, Rum Street, which suicidal drivers use to race to and from their jobs in downtown Cincinnati, cursing along in their death machines, playing "Insurance, Insurance, Who's Got the Insurance?" or "Demolition Derby" with their Pintos, Cobras, Beetles, Colts, Mustangs, Darts, Lancers, Cutlasses, Dusters and Furies.

I hear the cars go by. I hear the metal rasp and crunch. We have our invitation. I hear the shattered glass, the shouting, the honking and squealing of tires, the rifle shots off my marquee. I hear the disjointed hubcaps rolling up the spitty curbs. I hear the sirens of the ambulances, like those sirens that came for little Anne Frank. We'll be there, you can bet. But here in my movie house, it's mostly peace because I never stick my head out the roof like little Anne Frank did and I know every little part of this building. In the five and one half years that I've lived here I've come to know the water pipes, the gas pipes, the furnace and its ducts, the light bulbs, every wire that runs through the walls and to my lights. In the basement, in the walls, in the auditorium, in the lobby, in the projection booth of this old neighborhood theater where I fixed up a room right off the projection booth and where I sleep. I

cleaned up the place real good and use the toilet,
men's, down off the lobby to the left as you enter,
and rarely ever leave except for when I go out for
chili at the Bluebird Restaurant and when we go out
to buy groceries and light bulbs for the marquee from
Oscedo's Fruit and Food one block north up Rum
Street. My films are delivered and picked up by
armored car. I do my business by mail, even though
I have to give the mailman hazardous duty pay. My
assistants, Tracy Burdon and Ludovic Godescalc, live
in the basement and help me run the place. We all
work to clean the Omego I while I handle the films
and show the movies. She sells tickets and he takes
the tickets, tears them in two, makes and sells popcorn and sometimes some of the old, gooey Snickers
still left in the candy case from the previous owners
— we're worried now because we're about to run out
— to the five or six people who wander in in the
evenings, two performances, or during the matinees
on Saturdays and Sundays, to see "Dog Day Afternoon," "Freaks" or "The Exterminating Angel."

But that's not what my movie house is about. First
of all, when I got the place, I changed the name
right off. I had the marquee repainted yellow, I put
in all new light bulbs in the marquee, in the lobby
and in the auditorium, I cleaned the pigeon drop-
pings off the top of the marquee, I took down the
name, "Esquire," and I put up in big black letters
"Omega I" so that it would be my movie house
where I could show what I wanted to show and when
I wanted to show it. There's nothing symbolic about

the name I gave it. I just liked the sound of it — and still do. I knew some people would say, "Well, he named it that way because a movie house is a symbol of life." Or, "Life is a theater." That idiot response has to be tolerated, I guess, because there's no connection between my theater and what's outside its walls. In here there's peace and Sam Peckinpah, Stanley Kubrick, Roman Polanski and Milos Forman. Out there there's murder, rape, theft, politics, suicide, insanity, birth damage, learning disabilities, war, sexual perversion, disfigured and malformed people, automobiles with drivers, drunks with Mad Dog 20-20, baseball players with bats, a female novelist with a Winchester 30-30. The Omega I is something beyond all that. Life can't be like it. Life is not a theater and a theater is not life. My movie house takes me and Tracy and Ludovic way beyond what some half-educated pedant might gather from the name of my movie house as he or she drives past at fifty miles per hour dodging the dead bodies — dogs, cats, 'possums, rats, boys, girls, daddies, moms — that lie around on Rum Street until the ambulances with sirens like those that came for little Anne Frank come to pick them up. They can't know what the Omega I is by going to a movie once a week at the big theaters downtown. My theater takes me away. Takes me, and my helpers, into a warp where the woof, woof, woof of car wrecks, sirens, pedants and rifle bullets is but another frame flipped past a lighted and out of focus lens with a shutter cutting out the light forty-eight times per second so it won't flicker in our eyes.

After changing the name of the place and after unbolting mom's memorial chair from the floor of the auditorium and after bolting it down behind a film port in the projection booth, I got in my first film, "The Wild Bunch," and the invitation. I took the film up from the armored car, dodging three quick slugs into the marquee, to the projection booth, threaded it into the two projectors, turned down the house lights, called Ludovic and Tracy up from the basement where they were arranging their beds and shelves behind the furnace, their new home — they brought what they could, with smiles of thanksgiving, from their old cardboard shack behind the Water and Sand Funeral Home — and did what made the place worth $50,000, building, business and equipment included. I turned off the exit light down at the front of the auditorium. That light in movie houses always bothered me. I detested sitting to mom's left, downfront and strapped on, and watching "Gunfight at the O.K. Corral" or "The Gunfighter" and having that red goad just inside my peripheral vision. I hated sitting out "Gun Glory" and "The Gun that Won the West" with that red distraction galling me like the leather strap that hooked my right wrist to mom's left biceps. In my theater I turned it off, flipped on the first machine, focused the film. Sat down in mother's memorial chair, squinted out the film port at my own private showing in my own movie house. Ludovic and Tracy sat downfront, just their heads showing above the backs of the chairs, and ate popcorn while the ants swarmed over the scorpion. Rifle bullets thumped into the marquee. Glass splattered. Little Anne Frank opened the trap door in the roof of a Dutch spice shop and looked out at the sky. I sat straight up and thanked mother for it all. I also thanked Fay Wray and King Kong, without whom none of it would have been possible.

That was the beginning of life here, five and one half years ago, in our warp. Tracy, four feet tall and three hundred pounds, Ludovic, three feet and one inch tall, bald and hunchbacked, and me. We three with our squeaky voices together. They have a comfortable home and I have my room upstairs. I use the men's latrine, down off the lobby to the left as you enter the Omega I, my movie house, to bathe and shave and wash my long, straight black hair. There's no tub, but I wash with washrags and soap and it's not bad. We have a tub to wash our clothes in. And when we do wash them, we hang them over the empty orchestra pit in front of the stage to dry. But I enjoy my toilet, even though the crapper is in a very small booth and I can hardly get in it because I'm 6'9" and weigh 166 pounds. I especially enjoy it because while I'm carrying on my cleaning I can read the graffiti which I encourage and which I sometimes write myself. I'm not sure which of them are mine, most of the time, and I never remove any of them. I leave a felt marking pen hanging on a string next to the wash basin so that customers can add, "Laurel is Hardy," "Rin Tin Tin Loves Lassie," "My Friend Flicka eats hay," "Cheetah sucks Jane." Mine include: "The Gunslinger wore tight pants," "The Good, The Bad and the Ugly are all around you," "Every day is a good day for a hanging" and "How Green Was My Valley." Once when there was no more toilet paper, someone wrote on the leftover cardboard reel, "Gone with the Wind."

There's peace in the Omega I except that once a year I replace the burnt out light bulbs in the auditorium ceiling. Tracy gets out the thirty foot ladder and sets it up among the seats and I ascend, shaking and sweating, to the gray ceiling. It's hard work for Tracy and I worry because I think she might hurt herself lifting that ladder. Her withered right leg and her shriveling right arm don't seem to bother her too much and she says she doesn't mind too much. She says that it helps her get some of her 300 lbs. off her tiny frame. She sweats a lot getting that ladder up and then sweats some more holding it while I go up slowly, looking down into the empty space where mom's memorial chair once was, feeling the ladder wobbling under me holding the blue tinted light bulbs. I take two in case I drop one and when I make it to the top, I overcome my nervousness and acrophobia — I feel like fainting — by thinking of Clark Gable's mustache, a race between Trigger, Silver and Champion, Randolph Scott's smile, Hopalong Cassidy's black hat, Gabby Hayes' jokes, and I hear, way up there in the wet plaster air of the Omega I, the voice of Gary Cooper saying, "You can do it, Bruno. Yup, you can do it." I stand on top of the ladder in order to reach the ceiling while Jimmy Stewart nasals out, "That's fine, lad. Just fine." John Wayne snarls, "Unscrew the cover. Take out the burnt out bulb. Screw in the new one. Don't get them confused. Put the cover back on. Put the burnt out bulb in the box where you've taken out the good bulb. Don't open that trap door in the ceiling and stick your head out. Hold onto the ladder with your left hand and back down slowly." I don't argue with John. I do just as he tells me and when I get to the bottom of the ladder I sit down in one of the seats, usually on the aisle and in the center section, and tell Tracy, after giving her $100 as a bonus, in ones, for her bed, she can move the ladder to the next spot where, I can hardly face it, I can ascend again, quivering and sweating, into the dark air high above the seats and the silver screen.

Down in the basement, where Ludovic and Tracy live behind the furnace, it is peaceful also and warm in the Winter. They have two baby beds which I bought them at the Goodwill Store — good will, my ass; there's no good will out there — and some burlap sacks to cover with. Tracy puts a brown paper bag over her head in the Winter because the drafts down the cut stones in the foundation give her headaches. Ludovic, 3'1" tall and weighing sixty-five pounds, slides feetfirst into a burlap bag, his bag, like Tracy's, filled with old one dollar bills because new ones are too sticky, and Tracy tucks his crooked frame and hunched back in by tying the bag shut around his neck with a yellow ribbon woven through the jute. The rats never bother them and they say the whistling of the gas passing through the gas meter sings them to sleep. They hang their brown coveralls

on hangers which hang from the low joists and float
away among the paper money into never-never land
in their bare, scabby skin. The floor of the auditorium
is just over their heads and when the customers come
and go a fine dust sifts over them as they eat their
raw cabbage and their raw turnips or as they worship at their shrine set below the window well in the
front, the eastern wall, of the basement. Some light
gets down through that well because the well itself
is covered with a black steel grate. Passers-by drop
offerings to Kimoumgawasabi through the iron slats
of the grate set in the sidewalk. Gum wrappers, well
chewed gum, buttons, zippers, bottle caps, nickels,
empty Mad-Dog bottles, White Castle wrappers,
puke.

Twice each evening and at the beginning of each
matinee performance, as soon as the main feature begins, Ludovic and Tracy go down the stairs at the
east end of the basement. I don't particularly like it
that they leave the lobby untended for a few minutes,
but I can't stop them. I even join them sometimes,
when they invite me because I can't resist an invitation. We have speakers hooked into the basement and
we know what's going on in "Chinatown," "Rose-
mary's Baby," "Butch Cassidy and the Sundance
Kid" or "Soldier Blue" upstairs. They go down and
in the light that sifts down from the mercury vapor
lights in front of the Omega I they open the dirty
window and clean the offerings out and place them
in the bucket that stands before Kimoumgawasabi,
who squats on a wooden barrel. They close the win-

dow and kneel, chanting "Ti-ee, Ti-ee." They light
incense in the dim light that falls down over the
fetish with the large bird mounted on his back, a
bird, a gooney bird, whose beak points upward over
a stretched up neck and whose wooden wings spread
out sideways, three feet and one inch to the left and
four feet even to the right. The light descends down
the long, closed beak, past the button eyes held in by
wooden screws, down the post neck to the round
body. Along the leading edges of the great, open,
wooden wings. Over the skullcap and over his hairless head. Down over the cracks in the wood of his
beaked nose. His four arms wait in the shadows. Two
arms extend from each shoulder. The two upper arms
reach out with open hands, palm up, fingers spread,
to the supplicants. The two lower arms hold onto his
ankles as he squats. A large phallus rises from his
scarred crotch and reaches almost to his lipless
mouth. He looks as if he is about to kiss the head of
the phallus that has whorls carved in it that protrude
like large symmetrical warts. A large, gold wood
screw goes through his navel to hold him together
and to hold the bird on his back. The light falls over
his slit mouth, his beaked and nostrilless nose, his
mother-of-pearl eyes held in by screws. The gooney
bird leans his head back and guides the light down
over Kimoumgawasabi in the dim recesses of the
Omega I. Upstairs the guns begin to fire in "Bon-
nie and Clyde" or the sauna heats up in "The Virgin Spring." Feet scuffle on the floor. Gentle dust
falls through the incense smoke. We rise and go

back up. Tracy to the ticket window. Ludovic to the
candy counter. I to the projection booth. The silver
screen dances with the falling dead.

But now it is supper time. I'm hungry and I must,
before the first performance of this Friday evening,
go out. Time for a journey to the outside. Time for
trial. Time for endurance. Time to eat chili at the
Bluebird Restaurant. I yell down in my squeaky voice
to Ludovic and Tracy that I'm going and ask them
if they want to go or if they want me to bring them
something. They squeak back "no thanks." Yell
back that they have radishes and Gatorade for supper. Sweat starts. Light breaks through the glass
doors into the front of the lobby. I open them and
step out of the Omega I, step onto the ceramic tiles
behind the ticket booth. A bullet thumps into the
poster advertising "One Flew Over the Cuckoo's
Nest." Glass shatters at my feet. I blink my eyes
and run out from under the marquee, into the
setting sun, into the early headlights of the suicides
in their Rabbits, Falcons, Bobcats, Cougars, Jaguars,
Rattlesnakes, Rhinosceroses, Elephants, Brontosau-
ruses, Tyrannosauruses, Mothras, Godzillas, King
Kongs. Running north a little, I stop at the crosswalk and wait for the light to change. I look back at
the great bare north side of my movie house. It's blank
in the early, November evening. I cover one of my
lenses with my left hand. I switch on. I focus with my
right hand. I feel the sprockets catching the film and
moving it frame by frame between the hot light of
my head and the lens. The shutters spin. The sun-

light dims to a blue glow along the horizon. On the wall of the Omega I Walter Pidgeon, the world's greatest marksman, aims a rifle at Adolf Hitler. Walter pulls the trigger. There is a click. Walter snaps the fingers of his right hand offhandedly. Behind him two members of the SS are waiting. They arrest him for trying to kill Der Fuehrer. They take him away, but he escapes and comes back, by parachute, to finish the job.

The crosswalk light changes to "Walk." I run onto the street while the drivers snarl in their braking, slobber and gun their motors. I blink a lot and hope for the best and get it because I make it to the other side, as I've been doing for these five and one half years, in order to sit in the same booth. I can't sit on the low stools along the counter. My knees hit my chin if I try those squat blue vinyl and chrome fingers that cut off the circulation in my rump and legs. So I sit in a booth that has blue vinyl seats, a sugar jar, salt and pepper shakers, napkins pressed into a shiny metal frame and watch the feet come across the floor. A menu and glass of water appear, most of the crushed ice melted in the glass, in front of me. She says, "Do you want to order?" I say, "Yes. I'll have a bowl of chili bean, two coneys and a large Sprite." She says, "I'm not your waitress. She'll be here soon." I wait, along the wall covered with fake wood panelling, in my blue booth. Five minutes later I watch another pair of feet come across the linoleum. She says, "Sorry to keep you waiting." She puts down a napkin, spoon, knife and fork. I say, "That's all right. I'm in no hurry." She, in dark blue pants suit and with blue-black rotted teeth, takes a little green pad out of the pocket just over the appendix. "Would you like to order?" "Yes," I say, "I'll have a bowl of chili bean, two coneys and a large Sprite." She says, "Do you want onions on your coneys?" I say, "Yes," and she leaves. I wait. I feel the gum stuck to the bottom of the table. My knees are in it and some of it is stuck to my brown coveralls. I watch the feet come across the linoleum, the shoes badly walked-over to the outside. "We got no Sprite. We got Teem." "I'll take Teem." "Large or small?" "Large." The walked-over shoes and the rotted teeth fade out, a doorbell rings, a hand reaches down and opens it. There is a shot. A lady's high heels lie across the floor. Sirens ring through the open window, like those that came for little Anne Frank. The feet of the detectives wander around. Someone dusts for fingerprints. The body is covered with a white sheet and every once in a while someone lifts up a corner of the sheet and peeps under to see if the stiff is still there. Cameras flash. The newspaper men — you can tell them by the press passes stuck in their hatbands — are saying, in a pack, "Why don't you cops do something about these murders? How long are the citizens of Gooseville going to have to put up with this threat? The citizens can't sleep. Nobody's safe in this city." Jimmy Stewart picks up the phone. "Hello, chief? We've got trouble. Hallelujah McGee was just murdered. The citizens are up in arms. No

we haven't yet, chief. We think they're vacationing
in Monaco. No, I haven't said a word to the reporters.
Right, chief, mum's the word. Right. I'll take care of
it. No, no clues yet but we're checking. Right through
the heart. Fully clothed." I hook my fingers in the
gum stuck under the table and try to pull my pantleg loose. The feet walk up again. "Did you say
you wanted onions on your coneys?" "Yes, I want
onions on my coneys." "And will Teem be all right?
We got no Sprite." "I'll take Teem." The feet leave
and there is a calendar lying open to September. It
lies out in a field in front of bushes and then woods.
Leaves fall and cover the calendar. Wind blows. The
leaves whisk away and the pages of the calendar flip
from September to October, then November and then
December. Snow falls and covers everything, including the calendar. Winds blow away the snow and
the calendar flips slowly through January, February
and March as the snow slowly melts and flowers
appear, skies clear, trees and bushes green out. The
sun is shining and birds are singing as the calendar
flips through April and May and stops at June. A
bride and groom come walking down the country lane
as a bowl of chili bean appears under my nose and
I unhook my fingernails from the gum stuck under
the table of the booth. A soup spoon lies on another
paper napkin. Two coneys slide past my chin. There
is a small glass of Teem by my left hand. Two little
bags of oyster crackers lie in a little dish.

I take the soup spoon and wipe off the grease with
a paper napkin. The napkin crumbles and a paper

dust sticks to the spoon. I stir the chili because the
beans are all at the bottom of the dish. I break open
the little bags of crackers and pour them into the
chili. I stir them in and take a bite. The chili is cold.
I take the fork and wipe it with a paper napkin. Leaves
the fork covered with paper lint. I reach across
the bowl of chili and cut off part of a coney and
put it in my mouth. There are no onions on the coney.
I wave my gummy fingers to the rotten teeth. The
feet come across the linoleum again. I say, "Waitress, I'd like onions on my coneys." She says, "Oh,
I'm sorry. I thought you never took no onions on
your coneys." She picks up the two coneys and goes
back behind the counter. A telephone rings. A hand
reaches out to pick up the receiver. Fingers drum on
the table. A lady's voice says, "Hello. Yes, it's me. I
thought I told you never ever to call me again. Honey,
I'm never coming home again. You've been mean to
me for the last time. You can keep the children."
The hand, not holding the telephone, reaches down
and picks up a drink. The ice cubes clatter in the
glass. Susan Hayward says, "No, I'm not drinking a-
gain. I don't need your help anymore. I do not want to
fight with you. I just called to say that we're through.
In our eighteen years of marriage you've never once
treated me right. Cheap furs. Cheap jewelry. Frederick, I don't want to argue again. I know I called
and left a message. I'm tired of bickering. So don't
call me one more time. I don't want to hear from you
ever again. We're through and that's it. Give my
love to the children and tuck them in for me tonight.

Tell them their mother loves them. Tell them that someday they'll understand. Oh Frederick, why do we have to live this way? No, there is no other man. I've always loved only you. There can never be anyone else. I promise not to cry. No, I will not cry. I've already cried enough for one lifetime. No, I don't blame you. I'm the one at fault. I just couldn't live a lie any longer. It was me and my problems, not you or the mongoloid kids. You know how difficult it was for me when Helen was born with no arms and a pointed head. Of course you tried to make things better for me. But you never, never once, told me that your mother was born with her hands attached to her shoulders. Of course you talked about phocomelia. But how was I to know what that meant?" The two coneys, one with a bite missing, appear by my right shoulder. There are some onions on the coneys. I take up the greasy fork and take a bite from the unbitten coney. It's cold. I sip the Teem. It's watery and warm.

Now your coney is, technically, a sandwich. It is a bun, a wiener bun, slit lengthwise but not completely in two. A small, finger-like wiener is laid lengthwise inside the slit in the bun. Mustard is then rubbed onto the wiener and, usually, also on the bun. Chili, without beans, is then poured over the wiener and the mustard. The bun becomes a little gravy dish that holds the chili around and on top of the mustard and the wiener. Then a spoonful of chopped onions is dumped across the top of the chili. There you have your regular coney. If you want something other than that when you order a coney, you have to say so. Things like, "heavy mustard" or "no mustard," because lots of people don't like mustard on their coneys. I do. So I order regular coneys. And if you want some grated cheese on top of it all, you have to say, "I'll take two cheese coneys." Then you get a bun — or, in this case, two buns — slit lengthwise but not in two, with a fingery wiener laid in the crevice. Mustard is spread along the wiener lengthwise, usually with a small stick that looks like it came from an all-day sucker. Chili, without beans, is then slopped over it all so that the wiener floats in the mustard and chili and the bun becomes a gravy boat but with no gravy ladle for the wiener, the mustard and the chili. Onions are slapped on and float around in the chili. Then, a little furry cover of orange, grated cheese is combed over the chili, the wiener, the mustard and the bun. There you have your cheese coney. But you don't get that unless you order it special. Your regular coney has no cheese on it and that's what I always order. For the last five and one half years I've been ordering regular coneys. Once I did order "heavy onion" on my coneys. I got so many onions that I decided not to do that again. Your regular coney is my dinner.

I finish my food and wave to the rotted black teeth sticking out of the yellow gums. The feet come across the floor. She says, "Will that be all?" "Yes," I say, "and I'll have my check, please." She takes out the little green pad from her pocket just over her appendix, finds a pencil stuck to the pocket, and the feet go back to the glass counter by the cash register. She adds up the bill. She returns. She slides the green bill, face down, through the water and spilled chili on the formica top of the booth table. I pick it up, throw down a couple of dimes, unhook my brown coveralls from the gum, slide my cramped legs out of the booth, walk to the cash register and wait. It's a hot afternoon. The sun is "beating down." Dust and tumbleweeds roll along over the sand and past the cactuses. Suddenly a rider comes out of a large canyon, furiously whipping his horse that is lathered with sweat. Behind him you can see a pack of Indians howling and riding, without saddles, and whooping it up. The rider heads toward a fort that stands right out in the desert. The men on the walls see the dust in the distance. A bugle sounds. The big wooden gates in the front of the fort are flung open. The rider races in, jumps from his still running horse. The gates are flung shut and a huge plank is slid across the inside of the gate to seal out the Indians. The rider runs into the office of the commanding officer, salutes, throws some saddlebags on the desk. Beside the commanding officer is his daughter, Maureen O'Hara, in an off-the-shoulder evening gown. The commanding officer smokes his pipe. Fess Parker, in buckskin, with lots of fringes, salutes, and says, "Raining Fire and his renegade bucks have broken out of the reservation and are burning out the settlers along the Rio Bravo." Outside the gates, the Indians ride closer. A shot is fired. An Indian falls. Holding onto the reins of the spotted horse so

that the horse falls on its side too. The Indians ride
out of rifle range. They regroup. Ride whooping towards the gate of the fort. More shots. More Indians
fall sideways along with their horses. But the chief
rides in close. He throws a lance that sticks, straight
out, in the wooden gate. On the lance are eagle feathers and the dried scrotums of Mormons. Miss Pimples
appears in the next frame. Something's burning.
Maybe little Anne Frank. She says, "Sorry you had
to wait. Let's see now. What did you have?" I hand
her the little green bill and she says, "Was that a
bowl of chili bean, two coneys and a large Sprite?"
"Yes," I say. "But we don't have Sprite. We got
Teem." I say, "That's right. I forgot. It was a bowl
of chili bean, a small Teem and two coneys with
onions." "Oh," she says, " you had two regular
coneys." "Yes," I say, "two regular coneys with
onions." "Well," Miss Dandruff says, "you don't
have to order the onions separate when you order
regular coneys. They come with the coneys. If you
don't want no onions on your coneys then you have
to say so. Regular coneys always have onions on
them. That's what a regular coney is." Ronald Col-
man says, "There's a tobacconist right around the
corner." His friend says, "But I thought you said
you'd never been in Liverpool before?" Ronald removes his pipe from his mouth, stares at the change
in his palm. He's five cents short. He says, "You've
not given me the correct change." Miss Dandruff
says, "Well, let me add it all again. What did you
give me?" Ronald says, "I gave you two one dollar

bills." "Right," she says and hands him three one
dollar bills. He puts them in his pocket and walks
out of the Bluebird Restaurant ("Home Cooking.
Chili."). Greer Garson, sitting in the back booth by
the juke box, oggles him as he walks out. The "love
light" in her eyes turns into a single tear and Ronald
notices, for the first time, that she's grinding her
teeth and slobbering.

It is early evening when I leave the Bluebird. I blink
into the setting November sun and get set for my dash
across Rum Street. I stand by the pedestrian crossing and wait. No one stops. I wait some more. The
sun sinks lower. The rays become more dangerous.
When I look west across the street, spots dance over
the windshields, the bumpers, the pointed hoods and
the pointed heads of the maniac drivers. It's almost
time to begin the show. I lower one foot off the curb.
Leap back. A Starfire tries to put me in orbit. Blink,
blink. Zoom, zoom. Snarl, snarl. Honk, honk. Once
again off the slick slope of the curb. A Fiat gives me
an order. I retreat. Road Runners, Rabbits and Coy-
otes race by, go by. Go by! An opening appears. I
run into the street, off the spit-slicked curb, my
bowl of chili bean, two regular coneys with onions
and my small Teem bubbling out of my stomach and
up my throat. I rechew the wieners and swallow
them with my eyes locked on the double yellow line
down the middle of the street and my mind scanning
the triple yellow streak down my back. A Fury tries
to squash my heels. A bullet rings off his bumper.
A Swinger tries to push me up into the air so high,

up into the air so high, so high. A Tempest tries to blow me away. A Dasher challenges me to a footrace. A Duster tries to dust me off. Clanging of bullets off hoods and fenders. Rear windows shatter. Tail lights drop out. A Lancer tries to impale me. A Hornet tries to sting me. A Bobcat and a Cougar claw at my ass. A Cutlass tries to slice me up neatly. A Pinto, a Colt and a Mustang try to corral me in the second lane. A Dart follows me up onto the curbing on my side of Rum Street. "King's X," I scream as a Falcon flits down toward me and the marquee of my movie house, the Omega I. The doors are locked. A Gremlin sticks the lock and I panic. I get the doors open. Fall in. Locked just as a Super Beetle and a Cobra try to crawl over my threshold to chew on my size fifteen feet. Two bullets whop into the marquee. Glass floats down. Sweating and shaking, I dump my small Teem, my bowl of chili bean and my two regular coneys, with onions, on the octagonal tiles of my fainting.

I come to. But why, I wonder. I think of the invitation and my R.S.V.P. Ludovic is mopping up the puke. Tracy has the three lights left on the marquee on. I smell popping popcorn. Outside, under the marquee, ten people wait in line for tickets to "Dr. Strangelove." I try to say something to Tracy, but she waves me gently down. I want to help with the mopping but Ludovic squeezes out the last of the chili into the bucket. I hear Tracy saying, "Get up into the booth. We've got big business tonight." I look out the doors towards the ticket booth. The customers are shrugging down into their coats to dodge the flying slugs and the falling glass. I rise and Tracy hustles out into the ticket booth with her hands over her eyes. She has a great fear of seeing the one that will get her. Ludovic puts away the mop and the bucket. He goes behind the old glass counter and gets ready to rip the tickets in half by greasing his fists with melted butter. I rise and go up into the projection booth. I switch on the red exit light because it's the law, even though the exit door opens over a pit full of trash. I switch on the tape player and hear "The Jupiter" roll out over the auditorium and watch as the ten customers wander into the 350 seats and take ten minutes choosing where to sit. One wants to sit where mom's memorial seat once was. I smile and hope he'll try. I open the curtains. I dim the house lights. I turn down the music. Blue glow along the bottom of the silver screen. "No smoking please." I squeeze out the blue glow. Switch on. My light points out over the raised heads of the audience. Action. And the great silver penises of the U.S. Air Force glide out over "Try a Little Tenderness." I shorten my lens to focus the film. The shadows flick out from my port. Mom's chair is grainy and hairy. My shadows play through the motes and the ascending cigarette smoke.

During the first showing, fifteen more customers wander into and around the auditorium and when I close the curtains on the exploding atomic bombs, turn on "The Haffner" and turn up the lights between showings and wander down to the lobby, Ludovic is making more popcorn and opening a box of Snickers which he found under the counter among the dust and grease and putting them into the candy case. It's the first new candy I can remember, even though the wrappers are torn and the chocolate cracked. Outside, he says, are twenty-five customers waiting in the ricocheting bullets and falling glass. It's an evening of business triumph with no casualties so far. We're making money and we're happy. Busy bodies making entertainment. Busy selves making people happy. Feeding them first class popcorn. Serving them stale Snickers. Presenting to them a great film inside the Omega I, my theater, my movie house. Even the sniper doesn't worry us on this one evening when Rum Street seems quieter than usual. So far no sirens. So far no dead on the asphalt. So far no blood in the sewer drains. A quiet world out there. I think I hear a bird. After the end of the second showing, after the forty-two people leave — we've sold fifty-six tickets in all — I turn off the lights. Close the lids over the lenses. Close the curtain over the silver screen. Turn off all the switches, including all lights. And walk around with my flashlight. Ludovic and Tracy have gone down to their basement and I hear them squeaking their late obeisance to Kimoumgawsabi. I hear them scraping in the offerings under the grate in the sidewalk. I hope they have enough light. I know they have candles and that's why I've cleaned the basement so carefully. I don't want any fires. Then, finally, I hear them chuckling and tickling as they crawl into their burlap sacks full of money for the night. Behind the furnace. At the other end of the cellar from their fetish. I squeak down, "Pleasant dreams." And they call back, "Good night, Bruno. We love you," in their high, squeaky voices.

Sometimes at night when "Viva Zapata!" or "The Night of the Hunter" is over and I can't sleep, I go down into the auditorium and crawl around under the seats. When mom used to take me to those Saturday matinees for "Shane," "Stagecoach" or "Duel in the Sun," I always wondered what was under those seats. Strapped to mom I still wanted to look up and see what was stuck to the bottoms of the seats, what things were spilled on the floor, what leftovers followed an afternoon of "The OxBow Incident" or "High Noon." Usually I go down from my bedroom just off the projection booth into the pitch black auditorium, I take off my brown coveralls and hang them over a back seat and I get down and crawl out into that maze of chair legs, which is difficult for me because of my size and my big, beaked nose. But I make it around slowly, lying on my back and pulling myself along, scooting with my feet. To find the globs of gum sticking around, some of it obviously years old. I feel along. I find popcorn and taste it. Some of it is rancid. Some of it is greasy. It's hard to taste any salt on the spilt popcorn. I slide into spilled Coke and I lick my fingers to see if it is diet or not. I find Snickers with one bite taken out of them and that bite lying, half chewed, nearby. Sometimes I remember where certain ladies have sat. I crawl there.

I smell the seats from below. I feel around the floor
for lost coins, purses, glasses, pins, handkerchiefs,
wedding rings, zippers, knives. When my long
fingers find some wet, purple bubble gum still sticking and soft under a seat, I pull it loose and chew it
to taste the sweet lady and remember her, memo-
rialize her, who squirmed and cried through "Straw
Dogs," "McCabe and Mrs. Miller" or "On the
Beach." I blow light, purple bubbles up into the darkness and think that she was probably named Susan,
Judy, Doris, Maureen, Greer, Shirley, Vera, Ida,
Marilyn, Carole, Elizabeth, Marlene, Deanna, Katherine or Julie. When I can't taste the gum anymore,
I stick it back where I found it under the seat and
hope that she'll return for another chew. But tonight
I eschew the trip because I'm too tired. And to-
morrow we've got to go out for groceries and light
bulbs.

In the darkness, I grope back to my bed, a bed
made of two regular beds placed end to end. I crawl
under my canvas quilt, formerly a tent. I lay my
weighty head down, spreading my long black hair
out, softly onto my pillow, a gunny sack stuffed
with broken films. They crackle as I let the head
rest. One pokes through so I roll my head left away
from the point. It is good. I feel well. It is my time
to remember. I try even though I know that I will
weep. I recall. The leather straps on my wrists to hold
me close to the basement wall. I recall. Mom spoon-
ing oatmeal into my rotten teeth. I recall. Daddy
scooping my feces off the dirt floor and griping

about my manners. I know that I faced the wall and slept by the wall until I was sixteen. I recall. I weep. I pulled the rings from the wall and walked to the window with the iron bars over it. I looked out and saw things I'd never seen before. A tree. A flower. Grass. A dog. I pulled the window open by smashing the glass with my fist and then tearing the whole thing out of the frame. I crawled out. There was an explosion and something smashed into the window over my head. Glass fell around me as I stood, the leather straps and the iron rings with their bolts hanging from my wrists. I stood in the sunlight and blinked. More shots. More glass falling and leaves rocking down. Black spots ricocheted across my eyes. I saw the mailbox with names on it, James and Amy Ruckbein, and I heard someone shout, "Look out. Bruno's loose!" Somewhere the sirens rang, like those that came to get little Anne Frank, who stuck her head through the roof of the Dutch spice shop. Ten cops forced me down. I must remember. I was already full grown, with black hair down to my shoulders. I fought and wounded the cops with my leather straps and the iron rings and bolts attached to them. They were too strong. I'd been too long strapped motionless. I roll over to get away from a sharp piece of film in my pillow. My canvas from the Army surplus store is rough on my skin, but I have my heady strength from the basement wall. I recall in my own strength how I was chained to a bed which was chained to a cell wall. A doctor cut off my testicles. Mom cried. I cried. I learned to read at

Northview for five years while my hair fell out. At twenty-one, mom came for me. Dad had died of suicide. I remember clearly. After that I still stayed in the basement, unstrapped, except for Saturday afternoons when mom took me, my right hand strapped to her left arm, to the Esquire to see "The Covered Wagon," "My Darling Clementine," "The Desperadoes," "Gunsight Ridge," "Destry Rides Again," "The Indian Fighter," "Union Pacific," "Geronimo," "Pony Express," "When the Daltons Rode," "Welcome to Hard Times." To see "The Virginian," "The Westerner," "The Kansan," "Nevada," "Utah Blaine," "Wyoming," "Wichita," "Texas," "The Man from Laramie," "The Man from Colorado," "Dodge City," "Santa Fe Trail," "The Outcasts of Poker Flat," and " Cheyenne Autumn."

I counted time by Saturdays. Until I was forty-one and mom died watching King Kong finger Fay Wray. The ambulance came with its siren like those that came for little Anne Frank. I remember. The men in the white coats pulled mom loose from the gum under the seats. They cut the leather strap. They picked mom up from amidst her popcorn and spilled Diet Pepsi while I sat in the chair next to her, eating my popcorn, screaming at the projector operator to get on with the film because I wanted to see the ending of "King Kong." When mom had been hauled off, they showed the rest of the film, showed the bullets from the airplanes punching out the great ape until he fell not knowing what was up, and I went home satisfied. I didn't ask for my money back. I went home to my basement and waited by my wall, not strapped now, until the lawyers showed up six months later with that $200,000 and tried to talk me into putting it into stocks and bonds. I said "No!" and opened a bank account. A bullet smashed through a street light in broad daylight, just over my head, and glass fell about me as I walked to the Esquire. I walked right in and said, "I'll give you $50,000 for the whole place and all the equipment." I wrote out the check. And as Wilmer Gunsel walked out of the front doors, a bullet got him right in the middle of the forehead. He fell among the splintered glass and his splintered skull and the ambulance came for him with its siren like those that came for little Anne Frank. I roll over further onto my right side and curl into the canvas. The right side of my face is bleeding from film punctures. I feel drowsy. I wipe away the tears. I can't remember more now. I sleep.

It's Saturday morning and we've dawdled long enough. I've promised that we'll be there. I tell Tracy and Ludovic that it was exactly six years ago today that mom grabbed her breasts, fell and got stuck in the gum. That we need groceries, candy for the case, popcorn and light bulbs. We must leave the theater. It is 10:00 A.M. We know what will happen. I have $2000 cash in my pocket. We stand in the lobby, just back of the entry doors. We step through them and I turn to lock them. Tracy and Ludovic take hold of my hands and we walk under the marquee out onto the sidewalk. The shattered glass cuts our bare feet and we bleed. We blink in the bright light as the second floor window across the street over the Water and Sand Funeral Home shoots open. The head shoots out. Ludovic and Tracy hold on tight as we turn left towards Oscedo's Fruit and Food. We go slowly in our brown coveralls, me in the center, Ludovic on the inside by the yapping yard dogs. Tracy on the outside by the snot slickened gutters, walking carefully on the ball of her right foot, her heel lifted, her leg unstraightened. Her right forearm stuck straight out forward from the elbow and the right hand flapping at the end. She limps along under her oppressive fat and the second story lady shouts down, "Hey Tracy, shake a leg. Hey Bruno, she got a leg up on you? Hey Ludovic, you look like you need some legwork." We try to proceed with dignity under the pale, skinny, squint-eyed head of Martha Slug. I reach down to the limper and the hunchback, keep my chin up, my beaked nose arched and my long black hair straight, under her rumpless and titless meanness, under her red teeth, her rusty lips, her chest green with mold, her poisonous tongue. I, we, know she never laughs except when watching pain. We know she never sleeps. She has not been invited.

We go on under, "Just leg it out, folks. Hey Tracy, you look like you're on your last leg. You going to buy some leghorn chickens or a leg of lamb?" We go on even though we can hear something about milkleg, jakeleg, table leg, back leg, making a leg, leggings, front leg, first leg, pulling

someone's leg, no leg to stand on, legacy, a thou-
sand-legger, stretching one's legs. We go on. And we
know that Martha Slug knows what we are doing.
We know she knows what we are watching. We hear
gunshots and tinkling glass. We think it comes from
our movie house. We're not sure. We hear the cars
howling by. We hear the people spitting on the curbs.
We don't look back. We know she gnaws on her
arms. We know she eats pork. We know she shoots
damned good. We know she has written a novel.
Maybe about us.

    We go on in our brown coveralls with Omega I
stamped across the back to Oscedo's Fruit and Food
where we buy, for cash, one box of fresh Snickers,
fresh popcorn, fresh turnips, fresh cabbage, fresh
radishes, Gatorade, Twinkies (for me), Heineken
beer (for Ludovic), creamed herring (for Tracy), and
four cartons (twelve each) of light bulbs (for all of
us). We start back towards the Omega I, not holding
hands now because I have to carry the two sacks,
one of groceries and one of light bulbs, high over
the heads of my two sidekicks. Tracy says, "Mr.
Dillon, you reckon there'll be some gunplay?" Doc
Holliday says, "Sure ought to be." I stride on, my six-
guns loose in their holsters. We stride side by side
up the dusty streets of Dodge. Tracy on the inside
by the snapping yard dogs. Ludovic on the outside
by the spit-ridden curbs. Little Anne Frank lays her
head back on the antimacassar. I cock my shotgun
as we approach the O.K. Corral. We get into range.
The window shoots open. The frosty, squinty head

shoots out. "Hey Ludovic, where'd you play on the football team, in the backfield? What'd you play, fullback, halfback or quarterback? Your mother ought to get her money back. Ludovic, you get back-pay when you work for Bruno? You talk back to him? Ever give a piggyback ride?" We stumble, limp and lurk on. Somebody's hidden the corral. Ludovic stares down at the sidewalk. Tracy begins to cry. "Hey Ludovic, you get back pains? Do you live in the back room? Got a backboard? How about some Backgammon? Ever taken aback? Ever get your back up? Ever sit on a backporch? Play in a backyard? What's your background? Ever get a cutback?" We're in. I lock the doors. We know her hairy words. We know she shoots out the lights on the marquee. We know she put the bullet hole right in the center of the O of Omega. We hear the shots and the glass tinkling. Ludovic sweeps it up every day. I replace the bulbs. We know she stands behind her window and watches. We know she never sleeps. We suspect she never eats. We giggle when we think of her taking a shit. We make jokes about her sex life; tried it once and didn't like it in the ear, uses her rifle for other things, uses a magnet as a sanitary napkin. She stands at her window and stares into the setting sun. We love our own darkness.

I hurry up to the projection booth to put away the groceries because I know, as Ludovic and Tracy know, that it is almost time for their movie. We've dawdled too much of the morning away already and soon it will be matinee time and too late for our film.

I put the groceries in the cupboard in my room, eat
a Twinkie, and stumble back down to the lobby.
Ludovic and Tracy have finished their turnips. He
has also wiped the dust out of the candy case and
arranged the new box of Snickers beautifully. It's
the first fresh candy in five and one half years and
he has a little light shining on it to attract the customers. I give him $100 as a bonus — in ones for his
bed. Tracy has the broom and a dustpan to get the
glass. Ludovic brings the carton of bulbs, I carry
the broom and the dustpan and Tracy carries the
eight-foot stepladder. We go outside. Ludovic sweeps
up the glass from the sidewalk and puts it in a green
city trash can along the spitty curbing. Tracy opens
the ladder and sets it under the marquee. I climb up
two rungs and begin unscrewing the stubs of the
bulbs from the underside of the marquee. Tracy
holds a paper bag and I drop the pointed stubs from
my bleeding fingers into it. She hands me the new
bulbs. I screw forty-seven bulbs into their sockets
quickly and expertly. There are only forty-eight in
all on the marquee. I have a lot of practice at this
repair work. It is quiet. Our job is done and it is
our time now. Tracy carries the ladder and the remaining light bulb back into the lobby and I lock
the door as the window in the second floor of the
Water and Sand Funeral Home shoots open. We
watch the blue-black barrel of the Winchester
emerge like a telescope. We see the frosted hair, the
hairy fingers, the red eye squinting along the barrel.
Unsmiling. Three quick shots take down three new

bulbs. The glass clattters along the cracks in the sidewalk as we turn away. I go back up to my room and hear and smell the popcorn breaking in the lobby and I know that the reels are in the cans. I hear them opening the doors to the auditorium. I switch on the lights in the auditorium and turn on the Overture to "The Marriage of Figaro," Bruno Walter conducting. Ludovic and Tracy take seats in the front row and I know that they're waiting to be taken away and I am ready for that. I fold down the seat of mom's death chair, hang my wig of long, straight black hair on the light switch.

I know to open the projection ports. I stare out into the gloomy auditorium. I turn up the music and lower the lights slowly. The tape spins, reel to reel, and the Mozart washes over the erect seats, erect except for the two where Tracy and Ludovic sit down in the front row, eating popcorn, his right arm around her fat shoulders. And she reaching with her good left hand into the paper cup to pick out fistfuls of buttery, salted, fresh popcorn yellow and crunchy from the popper. I open the curtain as the house lights fade out completely and only the blue light glows below the silver screen. I flip off the exit light. Fading blue lights with my hand on the lever. The Mozart ends in the darkness and I announce that there is to be no smoking in the auditorium. "Please, if you must smoke, do so in the lobby." I lower mom's death seat and sit down. I strap my right wrist to the right armrest of the grainy and hairy chair. I snap the steel supply reel onto its spindle in my head, drop the covers from over my lenses. I thread the film from the main reel through the teeth of my sprockets behind my lenses. I draw the film down. Leave a loop below the lenses so that the soundhead can smoothly draw the film through my throat. I hook the leader of the film onto the take-up reel in my chest. When I switch on the light in my nitrogen-filled head, I feel the warm glow of my lamp as it reflects off the back of my skull. I lean close to the square hole to the theater. I open my eyes and the light jabs out the film port toward the screen. Switch on. My reels pull tight and the ratchets click the film in frantic jerks past the lenses. The Maltese cross spins. The shutters in my beaked nose whir. Black and white shadows flitter out of my eyes toward the silver screen. I focus carefully over the heads of Ludovic and Tracy. Concentrate. Sweat leaks from my leather skin. Intense heat behind the eyes. My hairless skull glows. The frames go by and on the silver screen the shadows turn into shapes. Figments into figures. Motes float across the light flicking from my eyes.

Ludovic and Tracy hoot and whistle as the title comes on: "The Filching of Eddie Punkbun." I feel it's the wrong title. I reverse the film and start again. "Fun and Games on the Serengeti." Hooting and whistling from the front row. Popcorn hurled at the screen. I reverse and start again. "Caterwauling on the Ohio." Howling, screaming, popcorn all over the screen. Butter blotches on the canvas. Ludovic ripping up seats and throwing them into the orchestra pit. Reverse. Start again. "The Care and Feeding of Little Anne Frank." Ludovic and Tracy move towards the curtain and the screen with fire. Panic in reverse. Panic starting again. Pale red screen. A huge bell, with a crack in it up the middle. A fat lady in a loincloth blams the bell, in slow motion, with a bent spoon. Fade out as Ludovic and Tracy sit down and put out their torches. On the screen: BLT Productions, Incorporated, presents "Omega Time." Fade out. Fade in: Bruno Ruckbein as Claude Bogart. Tracy Burdon as Jennifer Monroe. Ludovic Godescalc as Clark Cooper. From the novel by Martha Slug. Produced by David O. LeRoy. Directed by Cecil B. Eisenstein.

The credits fade out as some masked men, on horses, stop a train. They rob the passengers and ride off. Some more horsemen chase them. The bandits go to a saloon and flirt with the B-girls. The posse rides in and shoots the bandits. Some Teutonic knights in white tunics and with steel buckets over their heads ride by. There are slits in the buckets and on top of the buckets are steel eagles, claws or antlers. They ride out onto some ice. The ice breaks up and the men and horses thrash around for a while until they drown. A baby carriage rolls down a long flight of stone steps. A Mexican bandito says, "Bodges? We don't need no stinkin' bodges." A lousy Samurai warrior wanders along a desolate path. He scratches himself. He has a huge, curved, two-handed sword on his left side. He comes to a fork in the path, throws a stick into the air and walks in that direction pointed out by he stick. A man in short leather trunks swims along underwater with a blond lady who wears a leather swim suit. They climb up onto the bank of the river. It is a jungle. They wipe the water out of their hair and lie back on the grass. They embrace. A white feather floats slowly down. A heavy, busty blond jumps out of a flatbed truck and runs to where an exhausted mustang tugs at a lariat that ties him to a large tire. She cuts him loose. A hunchbacked man leaps from timber rafters onto a huge bell. There are handles on the bell. He hangs on, swinging the bell, pumping it until it clangs while he slobbers and howls. A man with tight, thick, blond curls plays a harp and mugs into the audience. A little man with a black mustache and a bowler hat sits and eats a shoe, cutting it neatly into bite-size pieces and belching. A thin girl opens the trap door in the roof of a Dutch spice store and looks out at the sky. A buttoned-down tank rattles through a narrow street, stops in front of a house. No one gets out of the tank. It stands a while and then drives off. Search lights spin their long beams off the sky. Black limousines line up to let their passengers out for a theater premiere. A limousine pulls up to the red carpet to the door. A woman with short blond hair and a black, filmy dress steps out. Her dress is caught in the door. When she walks away her skirt tears off and she enters the theater in her girdle and black hose. A bullet slams into the marquee over her head. Glass clatters but no one ducks. Men in tuxedos and top hats follow her into the theater, the Omega I. In the lobby there is a candy case with a box of fresh Snickers in it. Three bullets whine off the ticket booth. The limousines continue to pull up and celebrities step out into the spotlights. Newsmen flash their cameras. Autograph seekers strain at the ropes that hold them back. Police link arms to keep back the rabid fans. An ambulance races up, howling its siren like the sirens that came for little Anne Frank. An announcer stands with a microphone and interviews the guests of the Omega I as they enter. He has glass in his hair. He says, "Ladies and gentlemen of the U.S., this is the greatest night ever in the history of the motion picture industry. Tonight all eyes in this wonderful nation of ours are on this theater, the Omega I. All over the world people are anxiously awaiting the arrival of Claude Bogart, Jennifer Monroe and Clark Cooper for the premiere of their latest and greatest film, 'Epitaph for Rum Street.' We are expecting them momentarily. I think I see them approaching now. Yes, it is them in their yellow limousine. Oh, ladies and gentlemen, this place is a madhouse. These fans adore these great stars, these magnificent artists. I doubt that the police can control this crowd. Here they come now!" We step out of the yellow limousine onto the red carpet in front of the Omega I. Ludovic and I are dressed in eggshell-white tuxedoes with a silk stripe down the outside of each pantleg. We wear white top hats and white silk gloves. Tracy is dressed in a white, filmy floor-length gown with a white ribbon around

her waist. The crowd goes berserk. The police pro-
tect us as we approach the lobby, holding hands,
Tracy on my right, Ludovic on my left. Shattered
glass falls across our shoulders. We go on. The TV
cameras play over our scabby faces. We blink in the
spotlights. We approach the announcer. He says.
"Can you make a statement to the nation? All the
world has awaited your arrival. What can you say
this evening about this tremendous turnout?" Tracy
and Ludovic hold onto my scarred wrists as I lean
over to speak. My long black hair falls across my
mother of pearl eyes and my beaked nose. I say, in
my squeaky voice, "I promised my readers we'd come.
And we are here. On with the show!"

The Green
Bottle

E SEE HIM APPROACH the black iron fence whose spears and gate are taller than he. The gate is shiny. The spears are shiny. Their points are shiny. And all black. We see him who is called Sky-blue by his friends and Skyblue the Badass by his enemies, of whom there are two, mainly Hacker or Hacker and Spitter Hauck and Bums Puckitt. We see him who has the given name of Peter Solomon Seiltanzer and who has been since 1960 Dr. Seiltanzer (Ph.D. University of Michigan) or Peter or Pete or Peter Sol and Pete Sol or P.S. or P.S.S. And who is now in 1978 a forty-eight year old man with touches of gray in his silky blond hair and his blond eyebrows and mustache. Still slim

and still six feet tall and still straight in his posture. We see him walk up to the shiny gate, open it and walk up the steps of the Carnegie Library on south Main Street in Newton, Kansas, because he has been summoned by a member of the Harvey County Historical Society to the building which he notes is no longer a library but houses the records and bric-a-brac of the local historians, because he is Ph.D. and therefore a learned man and the historians need an opinion about a bottle that has three sheets of paper in it and the papers have something written on them in some language which the historians don't understand.

Dr. Pete Sol is wearing, we notice, a blue shirt with little pearl covered snaps instead of buttons on the two pockets over the breasts, down the front of the shirt and on the cuffs over the wrists. His belt is black leather and thick. His trousers are blue jeans. He has on his feet black penny loafers and white socks (100% cotton except 2% rayon) which he purchased at Malleis Store in Halstead when he bought, in all, twenty-seven pairs of cotton socks in packets of three and took all that were in stock in size thirteen.

We also know when and why Dr. Seiltanzer is in Newton. We know that it is a Saturday in the Memorial Day weekend in 1978. We know he has come to Newton, just arrived on Friday, from Cincinnati, Ohio, where he is a professor of English at the University of Cincinnati, to decorate and clean the false grave of his sister and only sibling, Grassgreen, Ticky,

Agatha Theresa Seiltanzer, who died August 13, 1976, at 4:32 A.M. and was cremated the next day in Wichita while her husband, Dirtbrown, Benjamin "Ben" Paul Kitzler, lay drunk on the porch behind their little house on Chilblain Street where they had retired and where Dr. Pete was supporting them and who had given Ben the money to get drunk or rather had promised him the money, on which promise Mr. Kitzler with a how-do borrowed five dollars from Alvin "Bums" Puckitt on the credit of that promise alone so we know, don't we, that Pete Seiltanzer's name is known in Newton, or maybe it was just the doctor label, the Ph.D. confused with M.D. I haven't yet decided why his name is known and trusted, but I know it is. And so do you. We also know the grave is false — there is a headstone, purchased by Skyblue, and a mound of dirt behind it in a cemetery plot also purchased by the Big S. in Greenwood Cemetery on east First Street where the good doctor's parents are also buried — because when the ashes of Agatha were returned from Wichita and given to Ben he had already gone out a second time and borrowed another five dollars, this time from Hacker Hauck, on the credit that that one promise from Dr. Seiltanzer gave him, a promise that Peter didn't make to Ben directly but through William Weary, a friend to Ben and a former neighbor to P.S., when he, Peter Solomon S., was called collect by Weary to tell him that his sister was dead.

Here's the scene: Mr. Benjamin Paul Kitzler, now a widower, lies drunk as a monk on Old Grand-Dad on the wooden and splintered boards of his back porch of the little house on Chilblain Street. William Weary, his drinking buddy, lies passed out on his back, cruciform, on the milkweed and bindweed in the backyard. He drinks Almaden Grenache Rose. Two half gallon bottles lie empty beside his trembling hands. A black Cadillac hearse pulls up in front of the little house with the peaked roofs, the two dormers and the two pine trees beside the crumbling brick walk to the collapsing front porch. The street is unpaved and there is a lot of dust. It is August 14, 1976. Hot. Dry and windy. Noontime. Bright Sun. Jim Bob Feigling steps out of the hearse. He is carrying a bronze canister in the shape of two praying hands, fingers straight, palm to palm. He walks up to the front door. The boards on the floor of the porch sag and squeak. He knocks. No one answers. He looks around. He walks around to the back of the house. He sees the empty Rose bottles. He sees two empty Old Grand-Dad bottles below the downspout. He sets the praying hands on an old, discarded icebox on the back porch. He shakes Ben. Ben rouses. Ben signs a paper. Lies back down and goes back to sleep. Jim Bob leaves, leaving the praying hands on the icebox. Evening comes. Full moon. Weary's face is covered with mosquitoes. Ants have crawled into Ben's shirt. He awakens. He stands. He helps Weary up and brushes off the mosquitoes. They both lean over and vomit into a bed of purple petunias. The flower bed is made out of an old steel tractor wheel with the spokes removed and then laid on its side. It's made from the rim. Ticky made it. She planted the petunias. They start into the house to wash up and get some water to drink. They see the praying hands. They wonder what it is. Ben sees that it is a canister and that there is a wide lid that screws off. He screws it off. Just ashes inside. He dumps the ashes on the petunias. He takes the canister inside. Rinses it out. Fills it with water and slurps from the tips of the praying fingers. Hands it to Weary. He slurps. The water tastes good. They agree that the bronze canister will make a good canteen for carrying water with them when they go fishing and need water to chase the Old Grand-Dad and the Almaden Grenache Rose. End of scene.

You wouldn't be able to tell where he bought the socks just by looking at his back as he turns the shiny brass doorknob on the big glass door and enters the ex-library building that was paid for by Andrew Carnegie to bring culture to the hicks. But I can tell you these things so that you won't have to worry about such trivia as to where Dr. Seiltanzer might get white, sized, all cotton socks in a time when artificial fibers and "fits all sizes" are so common. I can also tell you that Pete enters the library with reverence and fondness because he remembers the wonderful hours he spent there and the wonderful books he checked out and read. He remembers the coolness, the silence, the odor of old ladies and cheap paper. He remembers the children's librarian who always had good suggestions as to what to read and who one day told him that he should stop reading

Anna Sewell, Albert Payson Terhune, Will James,
Walter Farley, Eric Knight and Thomas C. Hinckle
and should go upstairs to the adult books. He remembers that he was in the seventh grade — we
know that it was actually the summer between the
sixth and seventh grades — and that he had just
finished reading the Bible cover to cover so he went
to the library, was told to go upstairs to the main
library which he did and he remembers ascending
the dry steps. He remembers the librarian staring at
him when he checked out *Daisy Miller* and *North
African Prelude*. She suggested Dickens, Scott, Cooper — good books for boys. Peter remembers that
the books were kept in closed stacks behind the
librarian's desk so you couldn't browse. You had to
use the card catalogue and call for the books so she
always knew what you were reading or wanted to
read. He remembers the smell of the librarian (lilac),
the smell of the room (encyclopedia), the dusty silence and the embarrassing squeaking of the oak
flooring as he walked out with his books and with
the librarian scowling at his back.

So we know why Agatha Theresa's grave is a
false grave and we know that a false grave costs
just as much as a real grave except for the vault, the
digging and fill-in costs, and we know that Peter
paid for it all because the husband, Ben, is indigent.
And we know that Dr. Seiltanzer is there from Cincinnati (TWA — first class) to decorate that grave
on a Memorial Day weekend in 1978. We also know
that he is in Newton for a second reason, and that

reason is to check out the welfare of his only niece, LaDonna Magdalene Kitzler, who was born retarded on March 2, 1942, and who has been in the Kansas State Home for the Mentally Retarded in Zimmerdale since December 21, 1958. Dr. Seiltanzer pays for her keep there — now $258 per month. He is also saving money for Benjamin's funeral.

So we know the two reasons Dr. Peter Seiltanzer, also Skyblue or Skyblue the Badass, is in Newton and we know his connections to the city and some of his background. We know enough to go on. But what about that bottle? We hear a scene in his Ramada Inn motel room, which is across the highway just east of Greenwood Cemetery. We hear first a three-headed Norelco electric razor buzzing the bristles off Pete's face. Next we hear the phone ring. The razor stops. The phone rings again. P.S. says aloud, "Why is that phone ringing? No one knows I'm here." The phone rings again. His shower clogs bang across the tile floor. He says, "Hello." And, "Yes, this is Dr. Seiltanzer. Yes. Yes. Yes. Yes, I'll be glad to look at the manuscripts. The old Carnegie Library on south Main Street? Oh yes, I remember it well. 2:00 P.M. That's fine. Can I just walk in? Yes, I have a rented car. Fine, see you then." We hear the phone put back on its cradle. We hear the clogs bang back across the tile floor. He wonders how she knew that he was in town, in the Ramada Inn and in which room. So do we. We hear the three-headed Norelco buzz again. We know that someone has called, a woman, and invited him to the library

but we don't know why. And we, like P.S.S., do not
know what those manscripts contain nor do we know
yet that they are in a green glass bottle and that the
bottle is corked shut with a cork.

We see him enter the brick building with the yellow trim, the high, fake half-columns beside the
door, a touch of the how-do to Greece. He walks up
three wooden steps and onto the oak floor that he
remembers so well. It squeaks as usual. But the books
he remembers are not there. Old newspapers. Pictures cover the walls. Hand tools lie about. Old bells.
Stacks of sale bills. Fruit jars and kitchen knives. Old
magazines. Dresses, shoes and hats. He walks to the
desk where the librarian scowled at him for checking
out Henry James and a book on the Berbers of North
Africa. There is a little chrome-plated service bell.
He hits it with his palm. It rings. An old lady comes
from behind a large stack of *National Geographics*.
He says, "I've come about the bottle." She says, "Oh,
you must be Peter Seiltanzer. You don't remember
me, do you?" He says, "No." "Well," she says, "I
was your fourth grade teacher at Ferdinand Elementary Grade School." He remembers her — believe me.
Especially how she used to smell. Lilac. Always
lilac. Even in mid-winter. The outline of her corset
under her tight dress. Her too white teeth. Her silk
stockings. Her black high heels. Her twisted hair in
black spirals. Her donkey voice. He says, "Oh my,
I do remember you. I'm sorry I didn't recognize you.
I've been away from Newton so long. You, I think,
whipped me once with a paddle." "Yes," she says,

"I did. But you were a sneaky little shit and you deserved to have your ass busted." We are amazed at what she says because it is not true. P.S. marvels at the language. What has happened, he wonders, to Ms. Bella Lacefield, the gracious and proper old maid who only blew her nose once on a handkerchief. "Let's see the bottle," he says. She says, "First I'll tell you how we came to get it here." They find two three-legged milking stools and sit down on them below a high clear window.

Ms. Lacefield's story: Herman Franklin Glastyn was one of the first settlers in Newton. He lived over the first saloon while he built a farm on a little hill near Sand Creek. Just west of the First Street bridge. Where the old packing plant used to be. The Santa Fe Railroad had already been put through and he worked part-time, sometimes, for the railroad. He did not remember the year he came here — he thought it was 1866 — but he did tell his son, who is the source of our information, that he remembered the buffalo coming to drink out of the creek. He also told his son, Franklin Herman Glastyn, that in September of 1886 he returned from a trip to Abilene, where he had proposed marriage to Phormia Lecat, daughter of the sheriff, and had been turned down, to find a team of white oxen standing in his farm yard. They were hitched to a covered wagon whose canvas was covered with paintings of dragons, angels, suns and two snakes around a stick. Inside the wagon he found two dead bodies, a man and a woman. He investigated their possessions and discovered that their names, painted on a sign for a medicine show, were Pinta Paluda and Pareunia Papilloma. A map indicated that they had been to California and were headed for Abilene. He also found a potato bug mandolin, 231 bottles of something called "Panchreston," and the big, green corked-up bottle with the three manuscripts inside. Herman Glastyn, then, according to his son, drove the white oxen and the wagon to what was to become Greenwood Cemetery and buried the two bodies together and left no marker on the single grave. According to Frank Glastyn, First Street now goes right over where those bodies were planted. Herman Glastyn kept the white oxen, the covered wagon with the golden decorations, the sign for the medicine show, the 231 bottles of Panchreston and the big green corked-up bottle. According to Frank, who says he remembers seeing all those things in his father's barn, the oxen died, the sign was used to start fires, the covered wagon broke apart and was used for firewood, the mandolin was traded to a Cheyenne Indian for two buffalo robes which we have in our Historical Society and the bottles of Panchreston started blowing up so they were broken up and buried. Only the bottle with the manuscripts survived. Frank says he found it in his father's barn when he died in 1902 and Frank himself took it and kept it in his barn on his farm over by Black Kettle Creek. As you may know, Franklin Herman Glastyn died in 1972. But before he died he donated the bottle and its history to the Harvey County Historical Society. Oddly enough, no one opened it until last Fall when I decided to look inside. There I found the manuscripts intact. They're in Greek, I think. End of Bella Louise Lacefield's story.

She rises from the three-legged milking stool and walks to a large, green metal cabinet. P.S. rises and follows. The oak slats in the floor squeak. Bella smells of lilac. She has given up corsets but P.S.S. can still see the outlines of her panties and her brassiere through her thin cotton blouse and skirt. She opens the cabinet. It buckles and clangs. She reaches up. Skyblue the Badass sees the bushes of black hair in her armpits. His eyes water in the stink. She lifts out a green jar. It is a cylinder thirteen inches tall. Diameter five inches. We are sure those are the correct measurements. We see that the jar has an opening on top. The opening is almost the same diameter as the jar and there is a big cork that corks up the bottle. Bella twists the cork out of the opening and hands the bottle to Skyblue. He reaches inside the bottle and pulls out one of the manuscripts. Each is rolled separately. He unrolls it. It is in Latin. Church Latin. There are no dates. Skyblue notes that the paper is laid paper. The script is Gothic. The ink is black. It is not palimpsest. The paper could be very old. It could be fake aged. He holds the paper up to the light from the window. There is no watermark in it. There is no reason for there to be a watermark in the paper. And we have no reason to worry about the lack of a date. We know the three sheets of manuscript will tell us what we need or want to

know. What they don't tell us we probably don't
need to know and it's probably none of our business anyway. A story is all right without what we
don't need to know. There'll be enough to make
sense of it. If not, we'll add something.

The first manuscript: (Let's call it manuscript A.
Dr. Peter Solomon Seiltanzer reading sotto voice. I
think Peter ought to sit down on that milking stool
to read, and Ms. Bella likewise, so they do. He reads
the Latin and let's have her scowl. He reads; she
scowls.) I, Dom Peter Paul Vareniky, on this Feast
Day of St. Expeditus in the Year of the Hakenkreuz,
do hereby attest to the truth of the narrative of the
finding, nourishing and educating of our Son in
Christ, the Father and the Holy Spirit, Fer Fio Lackland, and so record these truths for the guidance
and knowledge of said Fer Fio, named by us Lackland. (What shall we have Dom Vareniky record
about this Fer Fio and his finding, nourishing and
educating? I suggest a miracle. So let's have one.)
It was the Year of the Fachan, the Month of Guytrash. Bernard Oberycom, a peasant from Frsh in
the Scalp Mountains, and his wife, Plentiful, also a
peasant, a peasant wife, also from Frsh, were gathering wood (We don't need to know what they look
like or what kind of wood they were gathering)
along the River Boing when they heard sneezing.
The curious peasants searched along the bank, a-
mong the reeds, and found a cave dug into the bank.
When they approached the cave two river otters,
a male and a female, fiercely defended the entrance.

Bernard Oberycom took out his stenchmar (We have no idea of what that is) and killed both of the otters on the spot. Since it was the Month of Guytrash, their coats were full for the cold so he skinned them and kept the pelts. When they looked into the cave they saw a child lying on soft, dry grass. A pillow had been made from cattail seeds. There were fish bones lying around the bed. The child was dressed in rabbit fur boots, red silk trousers, a green linen shirt and a skyblue, woolen, knitted scarf was wrapped around his neck and head. On the shirt, over the left breast, was an escutcheon: black shield, red bar slanting down from left corner to right corner, gold star in center of bar, a silver gibbous moon in lower lefthand corner, in silver in the upper righthand corner "c'est vraiment incroyable." On the skyblue scarf, at each end just above the tassels, a solid gold sun with four big rays and eight small rays. (Now that we've seen the child we know he is of royal descent and that he was raised by two river otters. But what about that bottle?) When Bernard and Plentiful Oberycom, the curious peasants, stepped over the bloody carcasses of the dead otters and lifted the child from the cave they saw that he clutched a green, glass bottle shaped like a cylinder. (There it is.) In the top was a large cork that corked up the bottle. They could not get the cork out. (We can't let them open that bottle. It would ruin the story). The two devout and curious peasants brought the foundling and the unopened bottle to the Monastery of St. Dympna in the City of Merseburg. They then returned to Frsh in the Scalp Mountains with the otter pelts and were happy. (Ordinarily the simple, honest, curious peasants would rear the child. The child would be innocent, honest, hardworking, devout, respectful, brave and curious. When he became twenty-one he would get back his kingdom after severe trials and reward his foster parents abundantly.) We accepted the child and reared him in the monastery, although at first it was difficult because he communicated in a kind of sneezing and he licked his skin constantly. We had great difficulty getting him to stop his crawling-hop by which he traveled and to stop him from sliding down mud slides into the Exeter Brook. Our patience was, however, rewarded and soon Fer Fio Lackland, a last name suggested by Brother Lambert Simon Gorovei, became a quiet student and a strong worker for the monks of St. Dympna. We taught him not to look through keyholes and to clean up messes under tables. He was baptised on the Feast Day of St. Leonard of Porto Maurizio in the Year of Ghillie Dhu. His confirmation was on the same feast day in the Year of King Finvarra. He received training in the catechism. He confessed his sins with solemnity and without curiosity. That he grew no taller than three feet remains a mystery to us. Also his gnarled ears, his stubby fingers and toes, his flat nose, his bald head, his toothless mouth. All these things were told to me by Bernard Oberycom and Plentiful Oberycom of Frsh in the Scalp Mountains or were witnessed by me. Because Fer Fio Lackland is aetatis twenty-one and because he is preparing to depart from the Monastery of St. Dympna for his farm in the Valley of Althochdeutsche Lesebuch we present this account and attest it to be true and correct. We present one copy of this document to Fer Fio Lackland to supplement the note that he received in the green bottle at the time of his abandonment. One copy of this document will be placed in the green bottle which will be kept here at St. Dympna's. Signed: Dom Peter Paul Vareniky. Witnessed by: Brother Linus Andrew Bohnen-Pirogy, Brother Leonard Piroscky, Brother Gregory Peter Pflaumen-Keilchen. End of Manuscript A. P.S. hands the ms. to Ms. B.

We hear Ms. Bella ask Dr. Seiltanzer what the manuscript says. We hear him mumble that he doesn't understand it and must read the other manuscripts. They both stand up for a minute to stretch. He stretches; she pouts. They sit back down. Peter extracts manuscript A. (We have decided to call the manuscript read first manuscript B because we know now that one of the other manuscripts probably precedes it. So let's let P.S. read the second manuscript which we are now calling manuscript A. Dom Vareniky's ms. we'll call for the moment ms. B.) P.S.S. reads the Latin. Ms. Bella Lacefield walks out of the room. We hear the oak flooring squeaking and cracking. We hear a swishing sound in the room behind the desk. She will return soon, smelling of lilac even more strongly than before. Scowling and fidgeting even more than before. We know she knows she has lost control of the situation and that she wants to regain control. But, damn it, she can't read Latin and her former student can so for the moment he's in control and she must stalk, squirt, squat, scowl and fidget.

Peter removes the manuscript from the green bottle. There is one more sheet of paper in the bottle so that the labeling of the removed manuscript as manuscript A — not to be confused with the first ms. he read which we now call ms. B — is fortuitous. He holds ms. A up to the light. There is no watermark in the large sheet of paper. The paper is old. Not parchment. Not vellum. Nor palimpsest. But how old we don't know. Nor does Seiltanzer. And who cares? What difference does it make? The story can go on without us or him knowing how old the paper is that makes up ms. A. But Dr. Peter S. is a scholar and what he does is SOP. Dr. Seiltanzer pulls the second manuscript, although the order is fortuitous because he doesn't know what's on the remaining sheet, out of the green, cylindrical glass bottle and unrolls it. He automatically feels the paper and holds it up to the light to look for a watermark. There is none. There is one more sheet of paper in the bottle. For the moment we'll call that manuscript C.

Manuscript A as read by Dr. Seiltanzer (sotto voce) in the Harvey County Historical Society in Newton, Kansas, while he is in the town for the Memorial Day weekend of 1978 to decorate and clean the false grave of his only sister and only sibling, Agatha Theresa Kitzler, nee Seiltanzer, and to check up on his only niece who is retarded and is

confined to the Kansas State Home for the Mentally
Retarded in Zimmerdale and whose stay there is paid
for by P.S. Manuscript A: I, Leodgar, huntsman for
King Childeric in the Killmoulis Desert, do hereby
confess and acknowledge my complicity and guilt in
the removal of said king's firstborn son and do acknowledge and record that his queen of blessed memory, Amalburga, did also conspire and plot the removal of said son. I, Leodgar, a simple huntsman
and bachelor, a man of great size, a man of no ambi-
tion and less learning, was used and ordered to take
said son a great distance from the parents and to
kill him by cutting out his heart and returning said
heart to Queen Amalburga. Let me explain. It was
the Month of Joan the Wad in the Year of Bertilla
Boscardin when Queen Amalburga gave birth to her
first child and first son. But there was little happiness
in the royal household. We had all gone, we the
royal party, to the royal lodge at Thrsh in the Scalp
Mountains to escape the summer heat of the Killmoulis Desert. That's what the loyal subjects were
told. It was announced by the town crier that the
king and queen would remove to the Scalps for the
Summer. It was not true. They went for the secret
birth of their first child whom they had agreed to
name Fer Fio if it was a son, something they greatly
feared, and Viviana if it was a daughter. Myself,
Leodgar the simple huntsman, and the queen's pri-
vate nurse, Odilia, who was born at the Kerroo
Clough on the Dark River, were the only servants
privy to the birth of the son, Fer Fio, on the Day of

the Black Laird in the Hour of Dunblane. The necessity of secrecy and the immediate removal of the child was the ancient curse, from time immemorial, and recited each year by Eilian of Garth Dorwen to travelers as they passed over the Hickathrift Bridge over the River Boing and entered the Killmoulis Desert in the Month of Churnmilk Peg. The curse states that "The firstborn son of A and C/ Must to the desert quietly/ Be taken lest pox and plague/ The chills and ague/ Strike the people in a fog." I here confess that I, Leodgar, simple and obedient huntsman for King Childeric and Queen Amalburga, was commanded and did obey said command to secretly slip out of the lodge at night in the Hour of the Grave-Sow with the child and travel a long distance and find an uninhabited area and there cut out the heart of the child, bury the corpse and return with the heart to Queen Amalburga. (We all know the story by now. We see how things are coming together and how the story is progressing. We are pleased. We are pleased for two reasons: 1. Coherence is emerging and 2. this story is very easy to write.) I carried the child, I confess, out into the Scalp Mountains, out into the cold night air. My heart broke. How could I, a simple huntsman, murder the innocent child? I took the weeping child to my cabin and unwrapped the burlap that had been his only covering, He was cold, wet and besoiled. I remembered and got out of my special oak chest the clothes that I was wearing when I was found abandoned, a baby abandoned on a mountainside not far from the lodge of King Adalbert and Queen Cuthberga, the parents of King Childeric. (We enjoy this twist in the story. It will not be explained because an explanation is not necessary for the tale. Nor will the simple huntsman be described.) I cleaned and dressed the boy, the discarded prince, the should-be future king. I put my pair of rabbit fur boots on his stubby feet. I put my red silk trousers over his stumpy legs. My green linen shirt over his stubby fingers and short arms, the shirt with the black shield over the left breast, the shield with the red bar slanting across with the gold star in the center and in the black the motto, "c'est vraiment incroyable." I wrapped his neck and head in my skyblue scarf that has the tassels and a gold sun with rays at each end of it. I then carried the flat-nosed, bald and toothless baby out of the Scalp Mountains and down into the plain of the River Boing. I abandoned the child along the river bank and wept as I walked away. But when I looked back for the last time, two river otters were hopping around the child, licking his skin and sneezing into his ears. On my way back to the royal lodge in the mountains, I killed a black goat, cut out his heart and returned with it to the queen. She smiled and thanked me and gave me ten gold throts which I here give to Brother Mesrop Bartholomew Zucker-Platzle of St. Dympna's for hearing my confession and transcribing it this day. I pray that the child was found by some simple, honest and curious peasants and reared as their own child. I pray that Fer Fio

might return in his future life and reclaim his birth-
right. To that end I left with the abandoned child the
green glass bottle that was with me when I was
found. In it I put a single piece of paper with the
child's name and the date of his birth and then
corked the bottle tight shut. I did not name the
parents. I pray to God the Father, the Son and the
Holy Ghost that my sins might be forgiven and I
pray for the repose of the unbaptized soul of the
child if he did not survive. Heard and transcribed
by me on this Day of Chaise-Dieu in the Year of
Tod-Lowery. Signed: Brother Mesrop Bartholomew
Zucker-Platzle. Witnessed by: Brother Peregrine
Matthias Tjieltje. Brother Cadoc Jude Porzeltje. End
of ms. A.

Ms. Bella Louise leans forward and takes the manuscript from Dr. P. She is becoming angry that he
tells her nothing. She reaches for the green jar, but
P.S.S. quickly slips out the third document. (We
should proceed immediately to the reading of that
third sheet of paper and not take time from the story
to say that Dr. Seiltanzer feels the paper to see how
good and how old it is. He holds the paper up to the
light to look for a watermark, as he has been trained.
He adjusts his glasses and reads on, sotto voce, in the
lilac stench and hiccups of Ms. Bella.) Manuscript C:
Valley of the Althochdeutsche Lesebuch Year of the
Dun Cow of Kirkham Month of Yallery Brown Hour
of John of Nepomuk To Dom Peter Paul Vareniky
Monastery of St. Dympna Merseburg on Exeter
Brook Dear Dom I have traveled the highroad from

Merseburg south away from the city of star-shine in
the Month of Melsh Dick and Tatterfoal past Graham
of Morphie and come to the Red Hill I have circled
the Red Hill and crossed the Exeter Brook to where
I have built my little stone house and taken as my
Phol Nancy Beltane my white pigs with the red ears
are doing well as is my mule Dererustica and my
stallion Whuppity Stoorie my garden behind my
house prospers but I write because of the first appearance of my Silver Champion which might be of
interest to you since you have kept the green glass
bottle with my records and I wish this letter to be
added to record my existence after leaving the monastery and your valuable finding nourishing and educating please cork it up with the rest because of my
isolation here among the inchworms the firethorn
and the pigs since leaving you the Fachan has har-
assed me I know I was born in the Year of the Fachan and the Month of Guytrash but the trouble became too much when the Fachan would pound on
my locked windowless door and yell out who bit the
camel in the south desert what is the distance from
here to there why don't fish have feathers where do
the skunks have their libraries and when can the sun
be called the moon days and days he came to pound
on the door Nancy lost weight I lost my nerve our
house shook and began to crumble until I slipped
out in the Hour of the Moondance crossed the Exeter Brook and the highroad to Merseburg ascended
the Red Hill and laid my little body face down in
the night light I looked deep into my skull recalled

the magical sayings of the brothers at St. Dympna's
called on my unknown parents my unknown lineage
listened to the whinnying of Whuppity Stoorie and
the haw-hawing of Dererustica checked the fire-
flies in the brook's bed threw dirt over my bald
head put my flat nose to the rocks closed my one
good gray eye and saw the mastiffs the purple light
in the cave the blood on the ground felt the world
turning until there he stood silver sandals silver robe
silver face silver hair silver sweat silver breath coming
from his silver mouth silver tears from his silver
eyes and said you can what you will your lineage is
sound your will is strong your mind is complete so
answer with a strong voice before the world wilts
before the gray mastiffs before the Fachan over-
comes all before the Muckle Wallawa fattens I rose
and returned to my windowless stone house I listened for the riddles I heard how must a man be
born to be bearable and I shouted through the latch
hole barren and I heard when shall the blind be
opened to the light and I shouted through the door's
crack when the pickled pigs' feet walk in the firethorn and I heard shouted why were flies invented
and I shouted to dry the slobbery paths of the poor
in spirit the voice ceased I ate my supper of por-
ridge and rampion that night I slept on the cold stone
slab with Nancy Beltane and our family began in
the darkness the next day in my garden the potatoes
were rising the cabbage bulged the barley and rye
greened out and the turnips glowed with surprise I
have heard that the mastiffs of the Muckle Wallawa

are coming but I am ready the journey is not fright-
ening now and I will bring again the greenness to the
Scalp Mountains and the scrunch to the Fachan and
the Muckle Wallawa pray for me now and at the
hour of my journey to the north light candles for me
and my Phol yours in the Holy Trinity Fer Fio Lackland.

We see Dr. Peter rise. We see Ms. Bella rise. He
rolls up the three sheets of paper and she returns
them to the green glass bottle. The wide cork is re-
corked. Dr. Seiltanzer says the manuscripts are nothing, that they are useless and a waste of his time.
Ms. Bella thanks him for coming and he walks away
across the squeaking oak flooring. He walks out the
big glass front door and north on Main Street. He
is hungry. He is interested in spite of all. Here our
story ends. But wait. We know many questions have
not been answered. Some unanswered questions: (1) Is
this story autobiographical? (2) Does Peter actually
have a Ph.D. from the University of Michigan? (3)
Does Dr. Peter Solomon Seiltanzer really teach English at the University of Cincinnati? (4) Were the
ashes of Agatha Theresa Seiltanzer dumped into a
petunia bed? (5) Is LaDonna Magdalene Kitzler retarded and does she reside at Peter's expense in a
home for the mentally deficient? (6) How did the
green glass bottle get from the Monastery of St.
Dympna in Merseburg into the hands of Pinta
Paluda and Pareunia Papilloma? (7) Why were they
carrying it and preserving it as they sold their medicine? (8) How many years passed from the birth of

Fer Fio to the opening of the bottle in the Harvey County Historical Society? (9) Could Dr. Seiltanzer read Latin? (10) Did Ms. Bella Lacefield write the manuscripts and then concoct the whole story so that she could see her former student? (11) Is there such a range of mountains as the Scalps? (12) Could a river otter give suck to a tiny child? (13) Why are the monks at St. Dympna's all named after German foods? (14) Why is Fer Fio's white mule named Dererustica? (15) What is the Fachan? (16) Why is time named in the world of Fer Fio? (17) What was the name of the black goat that the simple huntsman killed for its heart? (18) Why, after reading the manuscripts, did P.S.S. stop on the corner of Main and Fourth Streets in Newton, pause, light a Winston Lights cigarette and think of the sentence, "I awoke one morning last March, a year ago to the day, with the sun burning the back of my neck and my wife's ankles pressed into my ears and her fingers wrapped in my toes?" We can end the story now because we all know there is one answer to all these questions and we all know what it is.

The Art of Vietnam

WAS DOUBLY surprised when I received a letter from Kenneth "Ken" Mortney. First of all, I was surprised that I received a letter. I don't have any personal friends and haven't received letters in fourteen years. I don't write to anyone and I don't want anyone to write to me. Secondly, I was surprised to hear from Ken. It was thirteen years ago when I last saw him in Saigon and I haven't even thought about him since then. The last I remember speaking to him was when we were kicking Vietnamese off a helicopter so that we could get off the ground before the North Vietnamese got us. The last time I remember seeing his face was when we threw an old man out of the chopper at 200 feet.

When the letter arrived, I didn't open it. I put it on my dresser, behind the purple heart and my souvenir AK-47. I knew it would take me a few days to get around to it. When I opened it a week later, it was a Tuesday, which surprised me because it didn't feel like Tuesday to me. Things were even more disturbing because of the attention I had to pay in order to read the first line. Ken's handwriting is fine. It's just that I wasn't up to that much input on a Tuesday, Tuesday being a day when I try not to receive direct stimuli. Tuesday is a day when I emit stimuli. Wednesday is receiving day.

The next day, I read the letter. It started off all right: "Dear Dirk, Haven't seen you in years." Then it got ominous. "Why not come and visit me? I live just about 100 miles from Cincinnati. In your hometown Nixonville. I saw your mother the other day in the dry goods store and she gave me your address. She said she'd like to see you too since she's not seen you since you got back from Vietnam. She said it's been something like eighteen years since she's seen you. Come on up and I'll have my wife Tan Son cook us a real Vietnamese dinner and we can talk over old times. See you, old buddy. Kick the door shut. Ken."

When I got off my Honda GoldWing by Ken's front porch, it was 11:00 A.M. He was waiting for me. He was sitting and drinking a Hamm's beer and, without getting up, waved me to shut off my motor and get up on the porch. He sat there in an old automobile seat and held out his hand. It was Wednesday, so I shook it. He took a Hamm's out of the paper sack and popped open the tab. I sat down on an overturned bucket next to him and asked him

how he was. He said he was fine and said he thought
I wouldn't come. I told him I stopped in town to see
my mother and that's why I was a little late. I told
him it was Wednesday and so I could make it out
of the city. I didn't tell him my mother died five
years ago.

We reminisced about Khe San and Saigon. We
talked about the war, the only thing we had in common, while I got hungrier. At noon I said to Ken, "I
didn't know you married a Vietnamese woman.
When did you do that?" "Yes," he said, "I got married just before we left Saigon. You never saw her
and I never told you about it because I didn't want
to get you mad." "Why," I said, "should I get mad?"
"Well," Ken said, "you remember when we were on
that last chopper out of Saigon? She was on it. She
wasn't supposed to be there, but I got her on. That's
why we were overloaded."

When I asked about his wife, Ken said he had met
her in Lucky Jim's Place in Saigon. He had formally
married her and brought her to Nixonville. I asked
him if she liked it in a small town and he said she
liked it just fine. I asked him about our lunch and
he said that Tan Son was fixing it and that it would
be ready soon — if she was done with cleaning up
after her painting. I said, "Painting?" "Yes," he said,
"when she came to America she took up painting.
Come on in and I'll show you some of her work while
we're waiting. Just kick the door shut after you."
Ken got out of his car seat chair, picked up the paper
bag of beer cans and headed for the door.

When I went into the room I was thankful it was Wednesday because the walls were covered with paintings. I couldn't have handled it on a Tuesday. Paintings hung above the doors and windows. Even the ceiling was covered with paintings, each one nailed into the plaster. Each painting was white canvas on a stretcher with no outer frame. Each painting was made up of one to four lines drawn straight but at various angles to each other. Each painting was a single color. Each painting was different.

Ken stopped just inside the door and said, "Dirk, here's some of Tan Son's painting. She gives them all titles. This one's called 'The God of the Ears.' "

"Is this a joke?" I asked. "It's just two vertical brown lines crossed by two horizontal brown lines."

"It's no joke. It took her a month to paint it. She sat at her easel so pretty, mixed the paints, carefully timed each stroke, while I sat beside her and shook the tambourine. For four hours each day. She's real meticulous."

"You shook a tambourine for four hours?"

"Sure. She thinks it's oriental music. At least it's as near as I can get to it. It's the only thing that sets her creativity free. I tried other things like a kazoo, police whistles, cymbals, gongs, whoopee cushions, sirens. Nothing worked. She just sat and stared at the easel as if she didn't know what to do. Then I got the tambourine. I shook it for her for four hours a day for two weeks. Every five minutes struck the head with my knuckles. The rest of the time the cymbals going continually. All that time she just sat there and stared at the white canvas. I was about to give it up and try a Sousaphone, but then she reached out and touched the canvas. A week later she picked up the brush. A week after that she squeezed orange paint out of a tube and onto her palette. She dipped the brush. I shook harder. I said, 'Kick the door shut,' and she lifted the brush to the canvas. Her first strokes were tentative. From that Tuesday on she worked quietly for three more weeks. When she was done I asked her what the single orange line was called and she said it was called 'The God of the Eyes.' You can see it nailed up there on the ceiling, right in the middle of the room. That was the beginning."

I asked Ken if all the paintings were named after gods and he said they were. "You see," he said, "Tan Son thinks that all things are gods so that anything she paints is a picture of a god. A mouth is a god. A shoulder is a god. A B-52 is a god. Napalm is a god. A tambourine is a god. Wednesday is a god. Tuesday is a god. You and I are gods. And she is a god. Everything."

"You mean," I asked, "that she thinks B-52's and napalm are gods even though she was in Vietnam during the war?"

"Tan Son says there was no war. She says it never even happened. She says she never even heard of the war."

I stopped in front of a painting called "The God of the Skin." It was two horizontal white lines with a white line intersecting them at about a forty-five degree angle. I said, "Are you sure, Ken, that Tan Son never heard of the war? How could she not see it?"

"She was burned over her whole body."

"When was she burned so badly?" I asked.

"The day we left Saigon on the chopper."

"And she was on the chopper?"

"Of course she was. I hid her in my duffel bag and no one saw her get on for the trip to the carrier."

"You brought her all the way here in your duffel bag?"

"Yes," Ken said. "And I taught her to cook and paint and drink Hamm's beer. I taught her to sit on the porch and write letters. I taught her to eat grubs and crawdads. I taught her to smoke Winstons and to hang her paintings straight. I taught her the tambourine and the frying pan. I taught her to clean fish and sharpen knives. I taught her never to mix any colors. I taught her to kick the door shut."

I said, "Ken, I'm getting hungry. It's already after 1:00. Couldn't we eat?"

"It'll be ready soon. Here, have a smoke and a beer. That'll hold you off till you can get to the Burger King over on the highway. Sit down a bit and I'll play you a song on the tambourine. Tan Son'll enjoy it too. She might not even start dinner until I play her favorite song 'Down in the Valley.' She'll cook up a storm when she hears that."

We stood by the easel and smoked our Winstons and drank our Hamm's and it was then I noticed how high the easel was and how high the chair was. I noticed, as Ken lifted his cigarette to his mouth, that he had paint stains on his fingers.

"Ken," I said, "I've got to be going. I have to get back for Thursday. I have a juice harp lesson tomorrow and I need to practice. Thursday is my music day. Tuesday I emit. Wednesday I receive and on Thursday I create. I lift my soul on the day of Thor."

Ken put down his cigarette in an ashtray and set his beer on a table. He said, "You can't leave. We can't leave. We're overloaded. We got to get someone off."

"Ken," I said, "I'll get off. Just open the door and throw me out."

Ken grabbed me, pushed me to the door. He kicked it open and shoved me out. He kicked the door shut as I stumbled and fell down the steps. My hands were cut. I wiped them off with my handkerchief. I went to my Honda GoldWing and got out my helmet. I put an X and an O into both of the tick-tack-toe games painted in black on the sides of the helment. The bike was right by an open window and as I waited for the pain to go away I heard a tambourine start up among the paintings in the front room. It got louder and louder. There were pops as knuckles struck the skin head of the instrument. And then there was a voice singing, "Down in the valley, valley so low." I stood there and smelled the delicious aroma of cooked rice and fish. I got on my Honda, revved it good, and kicked up a rooster tail of dust the full length of Ken Mortney's driveway to the road.

Passage to India

LVIN BONEYARD couldn't speak dirty to his wife anymore because of his laryngectomy. He could regulate the volume of his amplifier, but he couldn't whisper or coo out his deepest feelings, even when it was raining. When he touched his amplifier to his throat and tried to say something touching, what came out sounded more like goats bleating or like police commands through a bullhorn. To compensate for his deficiency, for the last five years he had sat at home all day. He sat naked in the middle of the floor, his obese legs crossed, his fat face and bald head shining under the bare bulb, and thought of things to say through his amplifier, something to keep life interesting, something he might say to his non-existent children, something to say to his aging wife Alveena when he met her at the door when she returned home in the evening from her job of teaching Education at the University of Cincinnati, something to snarl into her ear as she slept. Something so that when he met her at the door he could take her into his lardy arms, sniff her musky perfume and say, "The voice of the thunder is the morning song of old age." Something so that when Alveena lay and snored away in the dark, he could roll close to her bony back, touch his amplifier to his throat and say into her ear, "Encase your syllogisms in the bark of the sambar." Something so that when she sat up right smart he could laugh through his horn and listen to her whimper in her drowsiness and fright, "Turn off the TV."

After twenty years of marriage, Alvin mostly felt contempt for Alveena. He pointed out to her that she walked and talked like his grandmother. He snapped the dark bags under her eyes with his right index finger and told her her face was falling off. He liked to run his little finger through her downy mustache and tell her that she needed a shave. He pointed out to her that she grew up in Cincinnati, attended a Cincinnati high school, got her B.A., M.A. and Ph.D. all from the University of Cincinnati. One night he brought her up real quick out of her blubbering dreams when he growled into her ear, "You are as parochial as an ankle." And then got her an hour later with, "You have all the intelligence of a sandal." He regularly accused Alveena of teaching

"Schizoid models for the pursuit of learning." He cheated her when they played "Monopoly" or "Gin." He cheated her when they played "Trivial Pursuit" by giving her wrong answers for her questions. When she lost and complained, he snarled out at full volume, "Your head is a cul de sac and your brain is a speeding oxcart about to hit the wall at the end of the street."

Part of his contempt for her was that they had no children. In the fifteen years of marriage before the amplifier, he whispered and coughed out that it was time for a family, but she said things like, "Later, Al. Later," and "Wait for the monsoon." After the laryngectomy he figured it was the radiation. Alvenna said, again and again, that it was because he didn't know how to talk to children, that he didn't know how to be a father. She said, as if it came from the chromosomes themselves, "You can't rear children in unrepeatable babble. Language patterns form the mind, inculcate great thought, deconstruct the will to grossness, make productive citizens out of unformed but malleable gurgling. How could we communicate if we all spoke in the recondite gibberish that leaps from your puny cerebrations? You think children are cockroaches? You think children are putty in the hands of a nincompoop?" When she said to him, "Language creates the parameters of normality," he switched to high and snarled, "Your thighs are like jade elephants."

During the first fifteen years of their marriage, while Dr. Alveena Boneyard lectured on the generation of linguistic concepts and the parameters of language, Alvin sat at home and read books, drank beer and smoked cigarettes. He figured that since he had not gone to high school he would educate himself. For the first five years he sat on the floor, his fat belly sticking out, his hair falling out, and read whatever his wife happened to bring home. In the next five years he used the public library. Then he found out he could use the university library and he read "The Waste Land," *The Golden Bough*, *Arabia Deserta*, *The Brothers Karamazov*, *War and Peace*, *The Flowers of Evil*, *Leaves of Grass*, *The Anabasis*, Hesiod's *Theogony*, *The Gilgamesh Epic*, "Genesis." He read anything at hand until he began to dream of going back to where mankind began, back to the Garden of Eden, back to beginnings just as he was, by reading, finding his way back through language. He read about the Tigris and Euphrates Rivers, the Shatt-al-Arab, the Land of Ur. He read all he could find on Mesopotamia, Egypt and the Holy Land.

At night, filled with his readings and his longing to return, he would lie by his tall wife and whisper to her how he longed for her, how lovely her body was, how his passion was beyond all telling. He whispered to her that her hair was like gold thread on a pillow of silver. He said her eyes were like blue peacocks in a valley of green grass. He said her breath was like the western winds that bring the spring rain. He whispered and cooed to her that he wanted to take her to the land of Sheherazade, to the first land, to where we all came from. While Alveena

snored and blubbered out her pedagogical nightmares,
he sighed and told her that they could go away and
discover what they were and how they came to be.
He coughed and said that in the beginnings there
could be a child. Until the operation and everything
changed. Until Alveena told him he was nuts and
that she wanted to sleep.

On Friday, December 14, 1984, the jade elephant
looked up from her breakfast of oatmeal, two poached
eggs, Sanka and chutney and said, "Mr. Boneyard,
your cybernetic bombast makes my heart into a
graveyard of ineluctable crap. You make my beauty
sleep into a tippytoeing through degeneration." Alvin
looked up from the hambone he was gnawing and
reached for his amplifier. It was not in his pocket.
He looked up again. Alveena wept and pointed to
the freezer in the refrigerator. At first he didn't understand. He was confused because he had never seen
Alveena weep, not even on their wedding night
when he told her that her naked body reminded him
of a chicken coop. Not even when he told her that
her navel looked like an ashtray. Not even when he
told her that she would be for him the vessel of ma-
ternity and that he would launch her by cracking a
bottle of champagne over her brow, which he tried
to do and broke her aquiline nose. Not even then
did she weep.

As her tears dropped into her chutney, Alveena
told Alvin that she had gone to the doctor the day
before. Alvin groped through his pockets for his
amplifier. She told him that the doctor told her that

she would have to live a different kind of life. She said that the doctor said that at forty-four a woman was no longer a Mt. Everest, which could be climbed over, have junk dumped down her sides, have pictures taken on top of her. She said that the doctor said, "You are no longer young at heart. Your vital systems are going on vacation. They are going on an expedition into uncharted seas, into Terra Incognita, where fire and ice will permeate your deepest proclivities." She wiped her tears, blew her nose. Alvin looked into the deep blue of her eyes and saw black horses dancing through black caves. He saw the horses dying one by one. He saw red acids rot them away until all that was left was a withered old man gnawing on a leg bone. He tried to see who the man was. He tried to see if the man was happy or if he had found satisfaction for his hunger. He felt uncomfortable because he could not see those things. And then he realized that Alveena was not there.

When Alveena came home in the middle of the afternoon, Alvin didn't have his lines ready. He felt flustered. He'd spent most of the day thawing out and warming up his amplifier. Because it hurt his throat to put the cold plastic against his skin he hadn't had time to prepare to welcome home his wrinkled bride. Alveena entered, smiled handsomely and led him to the kitchen table, to the tear-stained chutney, the cold Sanka, the shriveled poached eggs, the dried and cracked oatmeal. She sat him down and, standing across from him, announced that she was going to have a baby. Alvin said, "The stream that flows from the elbow is full of tin fish." "And," she said, "you will not be the father." Alvin said, "The waves that wash the liver circle the earth in the magnitude of their compensatory reverberations, always seeking a piece of the thigh." "Furthermore," she said, "I want twins." "The hair that thrives in the armpit is the garden of fleas that leap at the sound of the trumpet." "And further furthermore, the father will not be an American." "All sound that floods out in the universe turns into flocks of birds that migrate from Mars to Venus and back." "And my pregnancy begins this evening." "Lost handerchiefs, stolen shoes, misplaced mufflers, all end up in the pockets of the hungry."

Alveena walked to the door and looked back. She wiped a tear from her left eye and said, "Can't you ever say anything common?" Alvin clamped his fist shut and remarked, "The closed suitcase hides the will of congress until separate decrees wail from the Banseri."

Alveena marched into the bathroom. He heard her banging things around. Heard her come out, go into the bedroom and hum herself into her best clothes. He smelled the rush of perfume as she swished by. Heard her say, "Turn off the TV." Heard the door bang as she stomped out. Heard the motor roar as she whisked herself away to become, he imagined, pregnant from some foreign professor who lived in squalor at university expense.

When she was gone, Alvin felt a minor distress. For the first time in five years. It had never occurred

to him that what he said was not common. He had
come to believe that all language is common, that
what we say is acceptable in all instances. A thought
of purple fish in a jar of peanut butter was as natural to him as his toes. To say that naturally followed
and was not uncommon. To put the words "mulct,"
"pawky," "epiboly," "tabla" and "Griselda" all in the
same sentence seemed as reasonable and common to
him as the hair on the back of the hand. Bambi
trussed up and dropped from a helicopter into Dis-
neyland was to him a commonplace. To think of a
cobra letting the air out of tires on the cars of the
FBI was as natural as breathing. What he said was,
for him, thoughtless. It seemed to him that some
great universal mind was speaking through him. It
seemed to him that he was in touch with a force beyond his control. It seemed to him as if what he
thought was the leftover reverberations from the
Buddha. His language was his nature; it came from
first causes, from the first thought that was. It disturbed him that someone thought the first bang was
not common.

Alvin got up and went to the refrigerator, got out
two slices of rye bread and made a sandwich of sar-
dines, peanut butter, raw oysters, a cabbage leaf and
orange marmalade. He poured himself a glass of
buttermilk and sat down to eat. He was determined
to say something common, to say something to quiet
his discomfort, whatever that might be. He wondered
why interesting things might not be common. He
determined to practice and when Alveena returned,

as she surely would, pregnant or not, he would speak lines of perfect commonness. He realized that he would have to think more clearly than he ever had before. So he imagined Alveena, flushed with passion, sneaking into the front door of their house while he hid behind the drapes and practiced common lines. He imagined himself taking her in his arms, dabbing the droplets of sweat from her hot brow, and saying, "You are as beautiful as maggots in sour milk." He suspected right away that if he said that Alveena wouldn't think that common. He tried again. "You are as pretty as a squashed monkey on the freeway." He realized that wouldn't do either. "The third time is a charm," he thought and said, "You are more beautiful than the river that flows from the eyes of dead cows."

The third time wasn't a charm, so Alvin decided to pack it all in and go to bed. He walked into the bathroom and hummed himself into his pink pajamas with the red snails printed all over them. He hummed himself into the bedroom, knelt by the queen-size bed and said, "Oh Lord God, maker, dowse congress with the sweat of peppercorns and lead the president into the foramen magnum of Mahatma Gandhi. A-men." He hummed up from his knees, climbed into bed and covered himself with the glory of his childhood, a comforter tied with bits of green yarn and covered with pictures of snarling tigers.

He fell asleep quickly and dreamed that he was sleeping profoundly. He dreamed that he dreamed about the right stuff, felt cool as a cucumber as he

soared like an eagle. A great eagle soaring on the
wings of the wind, like an astronaut. When he
dreamed that he dreamed that he bailed out of the
eagle's mouth, past his claws, past the afterburner,
he floated down like a pillow, floating on the wings
of song, a song he remembered as beginning, "On
the shore dimly seen through the mists of the deep
where the foe's haughty host in dread silence re-
poses." Firmly planting both feet on his mother earth,
he ate the parachute ravenously, like a hog at the
trough, like an astronaut stepping onto a point in
time. On the moon, he dreamed, he awakened and
slept like a log, a rock, a tree, a bumblebee, a ptero-
dactyl.

Nightmares came in his dreamed awakening, nightmares of words in piles he tried to sort out. He
sweated. He labored like Sinbad. Sweating and working on, he knew that what he was looking for was
somewhere in the pile. He didn't know what it was,
but he knew perfectly well that it was there. He
found: "The bumbershoot is the zygoma of the Eo-
hippus." He found: "A baby's breath is the whirl-
wind of the hexachlorophenes," "A soul is the path
through the junkyard of the stars," "When the cows
come home the water fleas cover the earth with spit-
tle." He found: "You need an airhammer to break
bread with the whippersnappers," "Slicker than snot
on the toe of St. Peter" and "A $60,000 dress is the
cocoon of the wrinkle." The word was there. When he
found it, he fell to his knees and prayed, "Oh Lord,
bless Shakerley Marmion with hemidemisemiquavers"

and he dreamed that the nightmares ended. He
dreamed that he lay down beside still waters and
slept quietly and all dreaming ended.

When Alveena sneaked in the front door at 3:00
A.M., Alvin was sleeping quietly. She carefully closed
the door and set her package on the table. She unwrapped it and took out a bullhorn. Removing her
sandals, she walked into the bedroom and put the
bullhorn on high. She roared into Alvin's left ear,
"Your breath smells like the tongue of the water
buffalo that lives in a high rise." Alvin jumped up
right smart. In his fright and drowsiness, he reached
out to turn off the TV. He flipped on the lamp. He
saw that Alveena was wearing a pink sari. He saw
that she had a red spot in the middle of her forehead.
He put his amplifier to his throat and said, "You are
as pretty as a picture."

Alveena put down the bullhorn and helped him to
rise and stand trembling by the bed. She took him in
her skinny arms. She unbuttoned his pajamas and
removed them. She hugged him. Alvin heard thunder
and heard rain striking the window panes. She kissed
him on the spot just above the upper lip and just
under the nose. As a faint hint of curry rose into
Alvin's nostrils, she said, "Now you are fit to be a
father."

Narodny Rasprava

E RUSSIANS DON'T know how to murder people. We do it very clumsily. We don't have the bravado that Americans have. They can take a pistol, walk up to a man, look him right in the eye and shoot him and kill him without hesitation. They can take a knife and stick it into a man just where it will do the most harm. They can put their fingers around a throat and squeeze until the victim turns blue. We can't do that because we don't like to look at our victims. We don't like to see them plead, crawl, moan, squirm, spit blood and die. Oh I'm not talking about the Third Department and its secret police. I'm not speaking about the military forces, although we are very poor soldiers.

We pity life so much that we have our professional soldiers and our peasants do our killing for us. No Russian intellectual, for instance, can murder cleanly. Just look at the assassination of the Emperor Alexander II. What a clumsy affair. A bomb at the horses and guards on a Sunday. The Emperor had to get out of the carriage before his legs could be blown off. And the assassin got himself along with the royal legs. That's why we murderers are sent to Siberia. That's why I'm here in Petrovsky Zavod in the Transbaikal. For twelve years at hard labor followed by lifetime exile. And without Leporello.

The bells in the Cathedral of the Archangel Michael began to toll an hour ago and I knew the Emperor was dead. When I heard the bells, I was busy trying to rewrite my notes on dogs in religious belief, my main work which I took up again last week when I was released after ten years of labor camp. I went out into the muddy street of Petrovsky to hear the news. The starving dogs were barking and nipping at the running Mongols and Buryats. Everyone was running towards the post office where the telegraph messages came in. A wandering holy man, a starets, stood by the the road and held out his leather pouch. When I gave him no money, he cried out, "May your dog bite your testicles." The arrogance of them. At the post office, just a small log house, the captain of the prison guards cried out for silence and then read that Alexander II, Emperor of All the Russias, etc., etc., was dead by assassination. He reported that the assassins were killed or

captured and that suspects were being rounded up.
The message said that he was killed by bombs
thrown at his carriage and then at his legs when he
got out of the carriage. When the captain finished,
I called out, "Was it the Narodny Rasprava, the
People's Vengeance, that did it?" The captain laughed
and said, "A fool can't throw a bomb."

As I walked back along the road, a holy road because the Decembrists in exile had walked it too, I
recalled how in 1869 Nechayev had brought me into
the People's Vengeance. He needed me, he said, because to be a legitimate revolutionary committee a
committee had to have six members. There was
Nechayev, also called Pavlov, Uspensky, Nikolayev,
Kuznetsov, Ivanov, poor man, and myself Ivan Gav-
rilovich Prizhov. Nechayev-Pavlov said he needed me
because I could translate Marx into the Kievan dia-
lect. He needed me because of my studies of beg-
gars, holy fools and drunkards, because of my books
Poor People in Old Russia and *A History of Russian
Taverns*. He needed me because I, constantly drunk,
believed that all popular uprisings begin in alcohol
and thus I could speak to the lower depths of society.
When I spoke to him about my great work *The Dog
in the History of Human Beliefs*, not yet completed,
he sneered and said, "Study the dog that is in the
Winter Palace."

My job in the committee was to convert the lower
orders. Even though I was forty-two years old and
a drunk myself, I was assigned the mission of going
into the taverns, into the streets, into the slums to

contact and recruit criminals, drunks and religious fanatics to support the People's Vengeance. My God, can you imagine trying to convert the Old Believers to anything when they have for over 200 years died or gone underground because they think it's blasphemous to make the sign of the cross with three fingers instead of two? Can you convert to the People's Vengeance Old Believers, who barricaded themselves in their churches and burned themselves to death rather than give up the Old Slavic texts? Can you imagine trying to arouse to revolution a wandering holy man, a starets, who is illiterate and covered with lice? Can you imagine trying to awaken to armed revolt the Skoptsy, who believe that women are the source of all sin and therefore, to avoid temptation, castrate themselves? Can you have a revolution by eunuchs? Can you imagine trying to lift to rebellion the Khlytsy, who believe in sexual abstinence between husband and wife but who also believe in concubines, abortion and copulation with all other wives and husbands? Can you imagine trying to awaken the Holy Ghost Worshippers, who try to breathe deeply enough in their prayers to swallow the Holy Ghost? Can a revolution come from these air bags? Not to mention the street criminals, the illiterate former serfs and the uncomprehending peasants. The drunks I could handle. I spent long hours drinking with them and arguing social protest. I drank and argued until I fell to the floor. But to no avail. I gave my liver to the People's Vengeance, but no one followed my thought.

I was drunk when Nechayev told Uspensky, Nikolayev, Kuznetsov and myself that Ivanov was a police spy and that he must be killed. I didn't understand, but, like the others, I agreed. The plan was simple. On November 21, we five came together in Kuznetsov's apartment. Nikolayev went out and brought back Ivanov. Nechayev, Uspensky and Kuznetsov went in a cab to Petrovsky Park to prepare. Nikolayev and I took Ivan Ivanov to the park, but first I insisted that we stop at the Raskolniki Tavern for drinks. Three hours later, after five o'clock when it was dark, we took Ivanov to the park to see some printing equipment hidden in a grotto. When Nikolayev took Ivanov into the dark grotto, Nechayev jumped on Nikolayev, thinking him to be Ivanov. When Nechayev got the right man, Ivanov tried to flee, crying, "What have I done?" Nechayev was most clumsy in strangling Ivanov. Ivanov bit Nechayev's hand so badly he let go. In the struggle, Kuznetsov sat on Ivanov's legs, Nechayev sat on the chest and Nikolayev grabbed the throat. After Ivanov was dead, Nechayev shot him in the head. The body was weighted with bricks and shoved into a hole we chopped in the ice of the lake where I once tried to commit suicide. The body was found on November 25 and we were all arrested, all except Nechayev. We all confessed. Uspensky told the police, "Give Prizhov vodka and he will tell the true story." I did. Nechayev escaped but was arrested and stood trial in 1873 and was sent to the Alexis Ravelin in the Peter and Paul Fortress in St. Petersburg where he,

like all those sent there, will die. Two weks ago Uspensky was hanged by some of his fellow exiles. In
1871 my friend Feodor Dostoevsky published a novel
called *The Possessed* about the whole affair.

When I read the outline of my life to the court,
I began, "I have led a dog's life." Everyone laughed.
To me the whole thing was not funny because I was
thinking of my dog Leporello and how he once at-
tempted suicide with me. I was thinking of the day I
took Leporello in my arms and jumped into the lake
in Petrovsky Park to commit suicide. Leporello did
not whine or yipe. He accepted his imminent death
like any Russian dog, except that he swam around
and around in circles while I floated there and waited
for him to go under so that I would know when I
drowned that he too was no longer suffering. It was
my love for dogs that kept me afloat until some
passers-by pulled me out of the water. Leporello swam
out, shook the water out of his shaggy brown coat
and looked at me with pity. I was ashamed of myself,
so I took the dog home, wiped him dry, put on dry
clothes myself and took him and myself to the Three
Oranges Tavern where I drank a bottle of vodka and
he drank a dish of warm milk.

It was this same love of dogs that led me to start
my great work *The Dog in the History of Human
Beliefs*. It was a work for which my whole life had
prepared me because only dogs have ever shown me
any respect and loyalty. It is true that my life is like
that of a dog because in Russia dogs are treated like
all poor people are treated. They are not fed, they

are not combed and they have to live in the snow. No wonder they are so mean. No wonder they are so emaciated and dirty. No wonder my first volume of my book was an act of love. No wonder that the first inspiration for the book carried me up to the time of Christ. No wonder my cynical wife burned all my notes for my next volume when I was arrested. No wonder that no one wants to know that dogs are better than humans and that there is no belief in God unless there is a dog there to point the way.

After I was found guilty in 1871 along with the four other members of the People's Vengeance, I was sentenced to twelve years at hard labor and after that lifetime exile in Siberia. When I requested it the judge denied my request to take Leporello along. It was a heavy sentence but the journey to Petrovsky Zavod was even heavier. Eastward to Samara. Across the Volga and the Urals. Eastward through the empty forests of Siberia. Around the southern shore of Lake Baikal to Ulan Uhde and then to Petrovsky. Riding in filthy wagons. Walking in mud in our shackles and rags. The peasants' dogs snarling and nipping at our heels. The peasants crossing themselves with three fingers and pulling the dogs away and calling us "unfortunates." Handing us hard black bread and turnips. It was probably better than the Alexis Ravelin. Until ten years gone, I was released from the camp to live in Petrovsky Zavod until my death or until such time as the People's Vengeance might rise and take us back to Moscow and St. Petersburg to see the emperor's dogs die in the streets, no matter how clumsy the killing.

Now Alexander II, Emperor of All the Russias, etc., etc., etc., is dead. Blown apart by a Polish student in St. Petersburg. A pistol shot at close range missed him. Four pistol shots at close range missed him. The bomb set off under the wrong train didn't go off. The dynamite in the Winter palace detonated but hardly damaged the floor of the Emperor's dining room. He wasn't in the room anyway. The tunnel that was dug from the tea shop to under the street was discovered. March 1, 1881. A Sunday and they tried again. The Russian threw his bomb at the horses and guards. The Pole got the Emperor.

The bells are still tolling. The Emperor is dead. The revolution is coming. It was all so clumsy because we just don't know how to kill. But it was done and now Herzen, Bakunin and Marx will rise and there will be no more oppression, no more hunger, no more suffering. Serge Nechayev and the People's Vengeance will be justified. Holy Russia will throw off her chains. There will be no more aristocracy, no more war, no more prison camps in Siberia. There will be no more hospitals filled with the dying and insane. There will be no more crime in the streets. No suicide. No murder. The holy fools will shut up. I will finish my book. I will have plenty of vodka. And all the dogs will be fed.

My Latest Sun

T 8:30 THIS EVENING I called my brother-in-law Benjamin Paul "Dirtbrown" Kitzler in Newton, Kansas. I wanted to tell him that it was October 13, 1982, and his sixty-fifth birthday. I did it out of family feeling, I guess, because he's all the family I have left, except for his retarded daughter La Donna, who lives in Wheatfield Acres, which is a holding pen for retarded adults who are kept there until they die.

While the phone rang, I could see the old house that I rent for Ben on Chilblain Street. I could see the two big pine trees beside the crumbled, red brick sidewalk to the rotting porch. I could see the two dormers on the sagging roof. I could see the dead

weeds around the empty flower beds. I could imagine Ben getting up from the filthy couch where he
sleeps, dressed in the same pair of bib overalls that
he has worn for the last six years, ever since the
death of his wife, and my sister, Grassgreen, Agatha
Theresa. I could imagine him kicking aside the pile
of Almaden Grenache Rose bottles, slurping some
water from the praying hands urn that once held
Agatha's ashes, and stumbling to the phone.

When he picked up the phone and said "Hello,"
I said, "Ben, this is Skyblue. How are you?" Ben said,
"Skyblue, for heaven's sake. I was thinking about
you today. There's something in the *Kansan Newspaper* that might interest you." I clutched. I knew I
was about to get dragged back into one of those past
events that I have tried so hard to forget. I knew
that Dirtbrown had but to mention certain names
and I would relive the turmoil, the embarrassment,
the nausea of my early years. I was not wrong. Ben
said, "Just a moment. I have to find the newspaper."
I heard him shuffling the sheets. I heard and felt
the snowy wings. I waited for another of those memorial trials. My latest spirits began sinking low. I
told my wits to come and stand around me and pro-
tect me from my former home, my relatives and my
friends and a memory that can grind me around and
me having nothing to say about it. What I lived before I did not want to live again.

Ben read: "Officials at the Larned State Prison for
the Criminally Insane have requested that anyone
knowing the whereabouts of any relatives of Apollo

Romanov Puckitt please contact the prison at once. Anyone with information should call Mr. Francis McGreavey, Director, collect. Mr. Puckitt's last known living relatives were his wife Adeline Corinna Puckitt and their son Alvin. They are known to have resided in Topeka, Kansas, until March, 1945. The wife and son moved to Newton, Kansas, in April, 1945, and resided at 901 Nagol Street. Mr. Puckitt mailed one letter to that address in 1947 but it was returned unopened. After his admission to the Larned institution, Mr. Puckitt had no contact with and received no mail from his family. Police in Topeka have supplied the information that Apollo Romanov Puckitt was committed to the state institution after he raped and dismembered two four year old girls in Topeka, Kansas, on February 23, 1945. He was arrested, tried and declared criminally insane by the courts. He was an inmate at Larned from August 5, 1945. He passed away on October 9. His body will be held for six weeks or until claimed, whichever is sooner."

Ben put down the newspaper and said, "Skyblue, call and tell them you're a lost relative and claim the body." I said, "Why should I do that? He's nothing to me." Ben said, "He's something to me." I said, "What could he be to you? You never even saw him. He died before you ever knew his family existed. You never even met Alvin and Adeline and they only lived in Newton for less than a year. Their house at 901 Nagol has been torn down. The two big pine trees are gone. The side porch and the bench swing are

gone. Adeline's Bible verse signs in the front yard
are gone. Probably no one remembers them except
me." Ben said, "I knew you would. You don't forget
anything. I know you a lot more than you know and
I knew Adeline better than you know. You probably
remember that she used to work nights at the Harvey
House. I met her there. I fell in love with her. I was
miserable. She had the prettiest ears I've ever seen.
I used to drive in from the farm nights, play the
punchboards in the Santa Fe Cafe, drink a bottle of
wine and then go and sit at the counter of the restaurant in the Harvey House and watch her carry
dishes in and out of the swinging doors. You've got
to do it."

I was angry. I realized that Ben, a married man,
had been two-timing my sister after only four years
of marriage. That's why she always wanted me to
stay with her out on that stupid farm. I gave him
what he deserved. I lied. I said I would call. I knew
that in one day Ben would forget all about it and I
wouldn't have to say that I forgot the phone number,
no one answered or that the body had been claimed
already. I didn't remember to wish Ben a happy
birthday.

The newspaper was right. Mrs. Puckitt and her
son Alvin "Bums" Puckitt did move to Newton in
April, 1945. In fact, it was Sunday, April 1, 1945.
I know all this because I first saw them when I was
on my way home from Sunday School. I walked by
the house at the corner of Nagol and Eighth Street,
901 Nagol, the house the Whitesells had lived in and

which had been empty for a year, and there they sat
on the side porch in the bench swing, swinging,
Mrs. Puckitt's right arm around Alvin, and singing,
"Jesus, Savior, pilot me over life's tempestuous sea."
I walked by and then thought that I should see who
they were. I went up the front sidewalk from Nagol,
walked between the two big pine trees that flanked
the sidewalk and past the catalpas along the Eighth
Street side. I came up behind them and they stopped
singing when they saw me standing by the porch. I
said, "Hi. I'm Peter Seiltanzer. I live up the street at
917. People call me Skyblue." Mrs. Puckitt said,
"I'm Adeline Puckitt and this is my son Alvin. He's
called 'Bums' because he's so stupid. He doesn't
know anything and he can't learn anything. And
his father's dead so there's nothing I can do about
it." Bums didn't say anything so I said, "Bums, there's
a pigeon on your head." He jerked his right hand
up to grab it. I said, "April Fool." They didn't laugh
so I told them that I was fifteen years old and that
I went to Newton High School and that I would be
a Sophomore next year. Adeline stared and said,
"Blest be the tie that binds our belts around our
waists." And said that they were waiting for Mr.
Miller to bring their stuff from the station. She said
they'd moved to Newton because the Lord had given
her a job as a waitress at the Harvey House. She said
she planned to work and carry on her witness. It was
then I first noticed the three feet by three feet cardboard sign hung on the catalpa tree by the porch. It
read, "If thy right eye offend thee pluck it out." I

saw Miller coming down Eighth Street. His two ratty
brown horses, his wooden wagon held together by
wire, wheels leaning out. And I knew they must be
awfully poor.

That afternoon I went over to see how things were
going. Mrs. Puckitt was sitting on the swing again.
Swinging. Her lovely gray brown hair pulled back
into a bun. Her thin ears surrounded by thin hairs
that waved around her thin neck and in the opposite
direction she was swinging. Her glasses with octagonal lenses and bright gold arms hooked behind
those fine ears. Her thin nose, thin lips. Her blurry
gray eyes. Her cotton print dress all purple and
green. Her black, thick soled, thick heeled shoes.
Laced with twine. Coarse brown woolen stockings.
Her wedding band like a gold tourniquet around her
left middle finger. I asked where Alvin was and she
said, "Bums is out back putting his doves into the
chicken house." I walked around to the north side
of the house where the old chicken house leaned to
the east. I walked up to the broken door. I heard
Alvin reciting, "Pigs have four feet. Sheep have four
feet. Dogs have four feet. Cats have four feet." I
looked in. Bums was sitting in the dust by a crate
made of slats and chicken wire. Eight or ten pigeons
flew around the ceiling. Dust and small feathers sifted
down into my face. I went in and asked Bums why he
was reciting what he was and he said that his mother
made him learn something new every day or else
she would chastise him with a whip. He lifted his
blurry gray eyes, brushed back his brown hair, rub-

bed his eagle nose and asked me how I liked his pigeons. I said they looked like pigeons to me and
wondered how he would keep them in the shed. He
said he'd train them for a week and then they would
always return to the same place when they were set
free. That night Bums fell and broke his left wrist
while catching his pigeons in Mr. Doonie's hayloft.

A week later, I was home from a week on Dirtbrown's farm, a week of milking, scooping manure,
Spring plowing, comforting Grassgreen while Dirtbrown drank wine and played the punchboards. I went
over to see the Puckitts and see how things were going.
Bums, his arm in a cast, was up in a catalpa tree. He
had strung a long piece of clothesline wire from the
catalpa to one of the big pine trees by the sidewalk.
I yelled up at him and asked him what he was doing.
He said he was going to join the circus. He was
learning his act. He yelled down and asked if I
wanted to try it first. I said no and he showed me
the wheel with the handles on both sides. He yelled
out, "All men are created equal" and slid down the
wire, gathering speed, until he hit the pine tree and
fell, stunned, to the ground. Adeline rushed out of the
house. She was carrying a piece of broom handle
about three feet long. She looked down at the gasping
Bums. "What did I tell you to learn today?" He
whimpered, "All men are created equal." She looked
down upon her son and said, "He'll never debate
the doctors in the temple." I stepped back when she
pulled him to his feet and said, "Close your mouth
so your teeth won't fall out." In the house, she

gently washed and wiped the blood from the three cuts on Bums' forehead. While she bathed his wounds, she told me that she'd spent all day Saturday trying to teach Bums how to write sentences. All I could say was, "It's not his fault that punctuation exists."

I think the reason I saw Bums and Adeline mostly on Sundays was that she worked nights and had Sundays off so she didn't have to sleep all of that day. A May Sunday, for instance. I'm home for the day after a week of burning up on Dirtbrown's burnt-up farm. Bums' pigeons sitting on Mr. Doonie's barn. Adeline on the bench swing, swinging and singing, "Jesus bids us shine with a clear, pure light." Bums and I sitting on the side steps by the lilac bush and the rose trellis. He trying to memorize the "Pledge of Allegiance." Me laughing. Adeline rising from the bench, saying, "As Jesus said when he saw the multitude gathered at his feet, to hell with it. I'll dash him with a rod of wood." She picked up the broom handle. I jumped aside and Adeline yelled, "And there came a voice from heaven saying, 'kerboom.' " Blood in Bums' brown hair. His gray eyes bleary with tears. I standing and watching the beating and saying, "It's not his fault you have to talk people into defending their country." Adeline yelled between gasps, "A whip for the horse, a bridle for the ass, and a rod for the fool's back," and me yelling, "Which one is he?" and she, between blows, "He's all three."

I dreaded the beginning of high school in the Fall. I was right. For Bums, an eighth grader even though he was fifteen like me, schoolbooks were diagrams of insanity. Bums said, "A lot of learning will make me mad." I sat and patiently tried to help Bums with his study. But it always came down to Bible verses, Gospel songs and the broomstick club. I tried to help by telling Adeline that "It's not his fault that a syllogism has three parts." She said, "Whoever spares the rod hates her son. Bums, hold your nose shut so you won't bleed on the lilies." I pulled at her dress, held her arm back and said, "It's not his fault that long division was invented before he had anything to say about it." And she to Bums, "Now grab the ground to keep from falling." I said, "It's not his fault that parallel lines can't meet," and she, "I'll take this dog by the ears and meddle a little with him and he'll learn the ways of the righteous. Wiggle your ears, Bums, so I'll have something to shoot at." I tried, "It's not his fault the constellations were mapped before his birth," and got, "His merciful kindness is great toward us. Stand up straight so I won't have to swing so far." When I suggested, "It's not his fault that songs are written down in notes," she replied, "Why didn't he die in the womb? Bums, cross your legs so I won't kill my grandchildren."

It came to be amusing to watch him trying to memorize "The Star-Spangled Banner" and "America the Beautiful." I amused myself by trying to imagine what he imagined when he said, "On the shore dimly seen through the mists of the deep" and "stern impassioned stress." I cringed when I thought of him reading "A Christmas Carol" and "Evangeline." The Pythagorean theorem must have been a road map to hell. "The summer soldier and the sunshine patriot" must have been like playing Jacks out on the lid of a cesspool. His class project in Manual Training was a lidless coffin for Adeline. So it wasn't so bad when Bums, through an ad in a matchbook, took up taxidermy. I could tolerate the sliced up sparrows, robins, meadow larks, pigeons and owls. I could even understand his eating flies, mice, rats, 'possums, snakes and hawks so he could, as he said, "Strengthen himself with his mouth." It was the bomb that finally left me like a lamb dumb before his shearer.

It was a Sunday afternoon in early October, 1945. As I walked toward the Puckitt's garage, I passed the chicken house. I could hear the pigeons beating their white wings against the walls. I looked in. The pigeons' feet were tied down with twine. I went into the garage where Alvin was mixing carbon tetrachloride, ether and gasoline. I asked him what he was doing. He said he was making a bomb to blow up the Japanese. I said, "It's already been done with nuclear bombs." He turned his furry gray eyes to me, I felt the snowy wings pass over, and he said, "What's a nuclear bomb? I want to have one. How do you make it? I want the biggest Japanese killer there is so I can help Adeline fly away to Jesus." I said, "I can't explain it. I can't tell you how to make it. It's a government secret." He grabbed my blond hair, looked into my blue eyes, picked up a tire iron and said, "You know everything. You're real smart. Tell me how to make it or put on a hat so they'll be able to find your brains." I whimpered, "Alvin, it's not my fault that you can't split the atom." He began to shiver. He put the tire iron down. Stuffed cotton into a can and poured his mixture over the cotton. I heard Alvin say, "She says 'There is one God,' " as he lit the match and I ran for the door. I turned to see him burning around the neck and head. I ran to the clothesline and took down Adeline's Wonder Quilt. When the fire was out, I couldn't close my hands. In the hospital, they covered Alvin's head, chest and arms with bandages. All you could see of him above the waist was the brown wax in his ears, the scabs in his nostrils, the caked pus on his teeth and his blurry gray eyes glinting out like the evening sun off pigeon wings.

Early the next Monday I walked past the side porch of the house with the two pines by the front sidewalk. My hands and arms were bandaged up to the elbows. I was returning from Quilty's Grocery where I had purchased an orange for vitamin A and my second degree burns. Mrs. Adeline Corinna Puckitt sat in the bench swing and swung back and forth. Her thick black heels struck the floor at each backward pass so as to lift her and keep the swing going. She was singing loudly, "Life is like a mountain railroad." I stopped and joined in with the "Keep your hand upon the throttle and your eye upon the rail." She saw me and smiled. She called out, "Skyblue, for God's sake, stay with me a while.

You won't have me with you always." I walked up onto the porch. She stopped the swing. I said, "Peel my orange." She did and said, "Take. Eat. Gnaw this watery flesh." I did. I wiped my bandaged hands on my jeans and sat down next to her. She put her right arm around my shoulders. There was a big glob of dried blood and wax in her lovely right ear. Scratches all down the right side of her face. I dug out the glob with my right forefinger and flipped it into the dried-up lilac bush. We pushed off together. Her ear smelled like orange. The swing lifted up. Our feet clacked in unison as we struck the floor on each backward pass. We kicked our legs out together at the high point of each forward motion. Her black leather shoes and my white Converse All-Stars.

Mrs. Adeline began to tell me how gladly her husband Apollo bore his cross of military service. How he wore his U.S. Marine raiment with pride. How Alvin had been of his father and how his father wrote every week to his son to tell him to be a good student. Adeline said she wept and wailed greatly when Captain Apollo Romanov Puckitt boarded the Chief in Topeka and rode off in the Santa Fe train to vex the heathen in the Pacific Ocean. How a soldier in his legion had written to her and told how Captain Puckitt died leading his hosts up Mt. Suribachi to plant the American flag over the utterly destroyed enemies of God. Adeline wept. Our feet struck the floor for lifting the swing. She said, "They put away my husband in a grave on that island and Alvin was never the same again." She sang, and I sang along, "My latest sun is sinking fast. My race is nearly run. My strongest trials now are past. My triumph is begun. O, come, angel band, come and around me stand. O, bear me away on your snowy wings to my immortal home."

The October sun touched the horizon and shined into our angel faces as we swung toward it, just as it must have shined into the face of Captain Puckitt as he fixed his bayonet, led his troops up Mt. Suribachi and took a bullet in his Christian heart. The light glittered off the gold nosepiece and the gold arms of Adeline's glasses. The low rays raked through the leaves of the withered catalpas, the dried-up lilacs, the bare trellis on the west side of the porch. We swung in and out of the shadows, in and out of her memories of the dead soldier. Off to the north, a freight train whistled for clearance through the town. I could hear dogs barking over toward the rising stars. Alvin's flock of pigeons circled down in the dusk to their roost in Mr. Doonie's barn.

The Fairy Feller's
Master Stroke

MY INTEREST IN Richard Dadd began when I visited the Tate Gallery in London on June 21, 1985. There I saw his painting called "The Fairy Feller's Master Stroke." I think the proper word to describe my reaction to the painting is that I was "captivated." I don't like to use words like that but sometimes it is necessary to fall back on the slop language of popular novelists. They have a nasty way of preempting perfectly good words by using them repeatedly in describing intense emotional responses in critical situations. Their characters are captivated, get in a maelstrom, are aroused, are fated, feelings are rampant, they wend their way, hie them to, pluck flowers, shed a single tear and suffer agony. All those good words have been turned into jokes by fiction writers who can't think and don't understand the magic beyond words.

Because of those goofball writers, I must say that Richard Dadd's painting sucked me in because as you look at the painting you seem to be looking through some grass stalks and into a fairy world. "Fairy" is another perfectly good word that can't be used anymore. It's been trashed by sexual wantonness. And what you see in the small painting — 21¼ x 15½ inches, almost a miniature — is a world filled with fairy folk all watching a single event. In the foreground, a fairy feller dressed in brown leather has raised his stone ax to the highest point of the stroke and is about to bring the ax down upon a hazel nut. The fairy world arranged in a great circle around a central wizard who wears a hat with a large brim and a papal crown and who extends his left arm out to the left and has his right hand raised in blessing waits to see if the feller will crack the nut. All activity has stopped. This magic world focuses all its attention on the face of the axman whose back is to the viewer and whose face cannot be seen. We do not know why everyone is concentrating on the face and not on the ax or the nut. Richard Dadd painted the painting from the lower right-hand corner and painted up and out. The painting is said to be incomplete.

The remark about the incompleteness was in the gallery program and sucked me further into the maelstrom of Dick Dadd's life. It's impossible for anyone to look closely at "The Fairy Feller's Master Stroke" and not be interested in the painter. The program also said that the painting was painted in

Bethlem Hospital for the insane where Dick was
incarcerated after killing his father in Dadd's Hole
in Cobham Park. It was those two observations that
led me to my investigations. My interest was a-
roused. I could not refuse the impulses from that
fated meeting of Shylock Shalom and the fairy
feller. In London on that dark day I could not resist
trying to answer the two great questions that arose
impeccably among my mental lucubrations: (1) Did
Dick Dadd kill Dad Dadd in Dadd's Hole? and (2)
Is the painting incomplete? I hoped that both answers
would be no.

My investigations told me, at first, only what is
standard information. I read the standard biograph-
ical sketches and found out the official story. I read
that Dick Dadd was trained as a painter and tried to
be successful as a genre painter of fairies. Dick went
to sketch and paint on a trip to the Near East with
Sir Thomas Phillips and somewhere in Egypt became
deranged and wanted to kill the Pope. Dick heard
dim voices telling him to rid the world of demons.
When he returned to England, he went on an outing
with Dad Dadd to Cobham Park, dined on hard-
boiled eggs and ale at the Ship Inn, walked with Dad
Dadd to Dadd's Hole, drew a spring knife and dug
into Dad Dadd's back until Dad Dadd was dead
Dad. Dick then fled to France and headed for Austria to kill the emperor. While traveling in a dili-
gence, Dick drew out his razor and threatened a
passenger. Dick was arrested and sent back to England. There he was declared criminally insane and

incarcerated at the age of twenty-six in Bethlem
Hospital in St. George's Fields in Southwark. He remained there for twenty years. It was there he
painted "The Fairy Feller's Master Stroke" between
1855 and 1864. However, before he could complete
the painting he was transferred to the new Broad-
moor Hospital in Berkshire and spent the last twenty-two years of his life there, dying on January 8,
1886. He was buried on the asylum grounds. Nothing
special about all that. The case seemed obvious. Except that when the authorities opened Dick Dadd's
room after he supposedly killed Dad Dadd, they
found the shells of over three hundred eggs and 223
empty ale bottles. They also found drawings of his
friends, all with their throats slit.

My suspicions became rampant. I wended my way
to the archives of Bethlem Royal Hospital. After
being ordered to remove my gold crown with the four
points on it, I was escorted into the archives where
I was shown a brown folder with "Dadd, Richard
n.m.i." on its outside. I sorted through the usual
medical records, police records, birth records. Until
I found a small hand-written note by the Lord Chancellor's Visitor in Lunacy, Sir Edmund Drystone,
n.m.i. I put down my spear, pulled my brown cape
closer around my neck and read:

"My suspicions are aroused. N.B.: (1) Richard
Dadd owned no spring knife. (2) His razor was
dull and nicked. (3) Hardboiled eggs made Richard
Dadd ill. (4) He is unable to open a bottle of ale.
(5) He continually speaks of Oberon coming out

of the trees and bushes. (6) He keeps on saying, 'Come unto these yellow sands.' (7) Compare George William Dadd."

I copied the note, with permission, and searched on. And found it. A letter written by George William Dadd to Maria Elizabeth Dadd. It was dated November 5, 1868, and sent from Bethlem Hospital to Maria Elizabeth in the Royal Asylum in Aberdeen. In the letter, George William wrote that he knew that Dick Dadd and Dad Dadd were going on that outing to Cobham and that while they ate hard-boiled eggs and drank ale in the Ship Inn in Cobham he hid himself in the trees and bushes by Dadd's Hole, put on his Oberon costume, opened his spring knife and waited. When Dick and Dad wandered into Dadd's Hole, he stepped forward from the trees and bushes, said, "Come unto these yellow sands," raised his spring knife high above his right shoulder, swished it down and cracked open his Dad while Dick Dadd stared at his, George William Dadd's, face. George Dadd then told Dick Dadd to get to France, lent him an old razor and ten pounds for the boat from Dover, and told him to go and kill the emperor of Austria. George wrote that as soon as Dick departed, Titania came from the trees and bushes and led him safely back to London. That's all he told and didn't seem to know what happened after that.

The guard would not let me copy the letter, so, while he was having his tea, I hid it between the sole of my right foot and the sole of my silver-topped sandal, sauntered out and hied me to the British

Museum. Oh the novelists think they know irony, but they can never match what happens in everyday life. That's why they have to use all those funny words. I discovered that George William was Richard's younger brother. I discovered that George William was committed for insanity on August 31, 1843, just three days after August 28, 1843, the day when Richard presumably killed Dad Dadd. George William was put in Bethlem Hospital on September 13, 1843, and remained there until his death on November 6, 1868, one day after his letter to Maria Elizabeth, who was committed to the Royal Asylum in Aberdeen on June 30, 1863, and who died there on October 1, 1893. Another brother Stephen n.m.i. died insane in 1860.

With the note from the Lord Chancellor's Visitor in Lunacy and the letter from George William Dadd to Maria Elizabeth Dadd and with the coincidence of dates, I thought, "Now I have the proof that Dick did not kill Dad." Unfortunately, when I flew back to the U.S. my bags were searched at Heathrow Airport. When I asked the guard why I was being searched, he said that I looked suspicious. When I asked him why I looked suspicious he said that they were always suspicious of anyone dressed like Oberon. He even made me take off my gold crown and put down my spear because they would set off the metal detector. While the guards looked and felt under my yellow tunic, one of my bags disappeared. The letter and the note were in it.

As for the question in regard to the completeness
of the painting, the day I left for the U.S. I returned
to the Tate Gallery to look once more at "The Fairy
Feller's Master Stroke" for signs of incompleteness.
The guards came and stood by me as I ran my mag-
nifying glass over the surface. While they searched
my leather pouch for spring knives and hard-boiled
eggs, I noticed that the two women to the left in the
painting, the dancers with large calves and full
breasts, have little spots of blood on their shoes.
While the guards searched through my brown cape
for bottles of ale, I noticed that the two cavaliers on
the right have warts on their noses. While the guards
removed my silver-topped sandals to look for hidden
letters, I saw that the wizard in the center of the
painting is blind and that his hat size is seven and
one-eighths, the same size as mine. When I reached
to pluck the daisies in the painting, I saw that the
grasshopper blowing the trumpet in the upper left
of the painting has watery eyes. I could not see if
the axman has a black beard and a black mustache
like mine.

When I was thrown out of the Tate, my magnify-
ing glass broke and I groped along the pavement for
eggshells. Crawling along on my naked, brown knees,
I had my first adumbration — a word I've kept
just to describe that moment. I saw before me the
hem of a gray dress. I stood up, straightened my
crown and saluted with my spear. She stood there,
holding a baby. She was dressed in a long gray dress.
All gray. She wore a flat-brimmed straw hat. She had

emeralds in her bracelets. The little baby had on black shoes. As I recognized her from a painting by Richard Dadd, her auburn curls fluttered in the breeze, the red ribbons on her hat waved, the feather on the baby's hat floated above her pink dress and a golden light stabbed out from behind their heads. While Crazy Jane waved her branches and filled the sky with ravens, the lady in gray smiled her soft smile and said, "Come unto these yellow sands."

I followed her and she led me into a dark grotto. In the center of a fairy ring, a nude Titania lay on a white sheet. She was asleep. Three nude women attended her. Outside the fairy bower, nude youths danced off into the shadows. When I could see more clearly, I saw that Oberon lurked in the penumbra of the grotto. He held a flower, waiting to squeeze out its magic juice into Titania's eyes. Overhead, huge, black bat wings flapped to hold off the darkness and to cool the glowing queen. As I stood and listened, I heard the fairies in the fairy ring over Titania singing a tinkling little song about silver beards and golden yolks. I heard their shivering laughter and realized that I was in a taxi heading towards Heathrow Airport.

When I got back to my house on Bush-and-Bear Lane in Cincinnati, I spent two weeks trying to put my investigations into a coherent, written form. There was the unknown letter, now missing. There was the copy of the note, now missing. There was the scrutiny of the painting, not completed. There was the whole insane Dadd family, now dead. There was the woman in gray and the baby with the little black shoes, now departed. There was the goofy language of goofball novelists, always present and always getting in the way. It seemed that every word I wanted to use had been contaminated by being used in some lousy fiction. I realized that the most intense moment of my life could not be recorded properly because of the wanton irresponsibility of ding-a-ling writers.

I thought it all over and realized on June 21, 1986, that my investigations had been futile. Nothing could be proved, so I committed myself to a half gallon pitcher of martinis and a bucket of ice. I committed myself to a deck chair on my cypress deck in my backyard where raccoons forage at night, where gold-finches fight for my thistle seeds, where a fox came once and where moles drill through roots. I committed myself to the blue balloon flowers, the red salvia, the orange and yellow lantana. I thought, "The flowers of the yard are a stone ax. The day lilies are the trumpets of the unseen. The mock orange is the eye of a wizard. The petunias are the wheels of mystery. The zinnia is the raised hand of the roots. And the marigold is the hat of vision." I committed myself to the almost-full moon rising and dancing shadows across my eyes. I committed my-self to the day of Saturn, the brilliant Venus, the gentle breeze.

I sat on my deck in my quiet defeat. I wanted to be like a character in a bad novel and shed a single tear for those who have learned the agony of defeat.

But I realized that something was all wrong. Perhaps it was that word "agony." I sipped my tenth martini and realized that it was the word and I realized that, in fact, defeat can be comforting. I realized that if you lose often enough you no longer have to compete. There's a gentleness in not contending that appeals to the inquiring mind. To sit and meditate and know that the turmoil around you is nothing is to find a dandy way to peace. It is in peace that we find our answers and my answers came when I committed myself to loss.

The almost-full moon rose over the elms, the pin oaks, the sycamores, the box elders, the silver maples, the apple trees, the red jade crabapples. The moon arose and its light made of my backyard a world encircled by shadow. I seemed to sit in the center of a ring of adumbrations. I put on my Snowy River hat so that any passing fancies could dance out on the wide brim. I reached out my left arm and raised my right hand in benediction. The moonlight came on until I saw a man dressed in brown leather. His stone ax was raised to its apex over his right shoulder. The fairy folk surrounded him and stared at his face. Holding his ax aloft, the axman turned slowly until he was facing me. I looked into the soft lips and watery eyes of Richard Dadd.

I dropped my right hand. The ax swished down. There was a cracking and ripping. The hazel nut splintered open. Inside was a raw emerald egg. While the fairy feller kneeled, cracked open one end of the egg and sucked out its golden yolk, the fairy folk

fled into the adumbrations. I felt the movements on
the brim of my Snowy River hat. The Spanish dancers spun off into the curling vines. Queen Mab's
car of state, drawn by female centaurs, rolled toward
my triple crown. The female centaurs grunted in their
toil. The gnat coachman cracked his whip. Cupid and
Psyche shouted encouragement. The strapping fairy
footmen clapped their hands and chased them all
across the brim of my hat and into the night.

When the fairy folk had gone away into the um-
brage, the center of the lawn began to glow as if all
the moonlight had gathered there. Until I saw Puck
shining like a phosphorescent jellyfish beyond my
silver beard and my cypress deck. He raised his hands
and laughed because on my left Oberon walked from
the trees and bushes and on my right Titania walked
from the trees and the bushes. An Indian child held
up the train of her green robe. Oberon and Titania
met in the center of the lawn, touched spearpoints,
joined hands and bowed toward me. Moonlight
sparkled off their gold crowns. Puck leaped up,
pushed out his left arm straight to the left and
raised his right hand in benediction. He called out,
"Shylock Shalom, over hill and over dale, follow
now my sparkling trail. Raise your palette. Shine
your eyes. From right corner out of sight." A cloud
covered the almost-full moon, and Puck, Titania and
Oberon faded back into the shadows. I sucked down
my twelfth martini and knew that Dick Dadd did not
kill Dad Dadd in Dadd's Hole and I knew that the
painting was finished.

Elegy

N HOWDY DOODY VILLA, the afternoon schedule calls for newspaper reading at 2:30. The period is called "Cur-
rent Events." At 2:25 the attendants
come around, load us into our wheel-
chairs and push us to the rec. room.
Punjab comes into my room and says to my room-
mate, "OK, Joe. Time to find out who was in town
yesterday." If Joe Btfstlk is obstreperous, Punjab
says, "Joe, if you don't cooperate I'll take away your
cup of water." Joe murmurs, "Will someone help
me, please?" and then silence as he bumps into the
wheelchair. Punjab then comes to me and says,

"Willie, there's lots of buyers today who are looking for hot items. The economy's improving and if you got something to sell now's the time." He puts his big arms under me. I rise. I bend at the waist. I feel the canvas seat against my ninety-four year old back and legs. I feel dizzy as he whirls my wheelchair around and rushes me down the hall to hear the news.

We sit in the rec. room and wait. I know Joe is next to me because I can smell his urine-soaked clothes and I can hear the water spilling from his cup. I asked Porkie Pig once how we were seated and she said, "In order." I said, "What order?" She said, "In the order that you are domiciled." I asked why that order and she said it was so that the attendants would know if anyone was missing. I asked, "How could anyone be missing?" and I knew the answer. I knew that we were drawn up in two ranks in order to salute anyone who might have gone bad in the night and was removed before he had a chance to hear the day's catastrophes.

When Catherine the Great comes in to read the *Kansan Newspaper* there is always arguing. In the south line, Snow White and Little Orphan Annie want to hear the engagement announcements and the wedding write-ups. Pope John wants the church schedules. Tweetie Pie and Olive Oyl want the ads for sales in the clothing stores. Bashful and Happy want the weather report. Pogo wants the movies. Sneezy, Donald Duck, Daisy Mae and Tess Trueheart mumble in their drugs. On our side, the north

line, Quasimodo demands the obituaries and the
Dragon Lady and Gravel Gertie agree. Cabbage Patch
and Smurf want the automobile accidents. King
David wants to know if there is destruction in the
west and light bursting from the east. He wants to
know if the Beast from the Sea is at the city limits
and if the Whore of Babylon has arrived on Amtrak's
Southwest Limited. Sleepy, Grumpy, Doc and Dopey
hi-ho along and support our side. Joe Btfstlk says,
"Will someone help me, please?" and wants to know
who the out-of-town visitors have been. I suck in
my slobber from around my false teeth and ask for
the want ads.

Catherine the Great says, as she always says, "Now
people, we will have quiet or I won't read anything.
The paper will be read in order." She reads to us about
American soldiers blasted to bits in Lebanon. She
reads about American marines murdering Cubans in
Grenada. She reads about millions of dollars in aid
for El Salvador. She reads about Nancy Reagan getting a sixty thousand dollar dress and 200 thousand
dollars worth of dishes. She reads about the Rea-
gans on their California ranch and the preaching a-
bout excellence in education. She reads about mis-
siles and nuclear submarines, Cappie Weinberger's
star wars and waterhead Watt's selling of America.
The south side falls asleep. The north side sucks bits
of food from under their false teeth. Our legs grow
numb. We pick at our skin and wonder who those
people are and where those places are. We know only
that they are outside. We await the inside pages.

After thirty minutes of reading, Catherine finally
gets to my favorite part of the paper, the want ads.
I like those ads because I think our culture is de-
fined by what we buy from and what we sell to each
other. I don't mean the kinds of things bought and
sold in the Safeway or Dillon Supermarkets. I don't
mean what we buy in Woolworth's or J.C. Penney's
stores, in Toev's Men's and Boy's Wear or the Et-
Cetera Shop. I mean what we personally, face to face,
buy and sell. We go to auctions and bid on broken
chairs and Depression Glass. We advertise our old
bicycles, our Mason jars, our cracked crocks, pieces
of old harness, old Bibles, our granite pitchers. The
objects are worthless. Everyone knows that. It's the
human contact that is exciting. You see the person
who swindles you. You see the person you swindle.
Things and money pass from dishonest hand to dishonest hand. You laugh when you seal the bargain
with a handshake. It's got to be thrilling to see your
neighbor, a member of your church or a member of
the PTA pay fifteen dollars for a little toy cast-iron
plow that you bought for twenty-five cents twenty
years ago. It's got to be thrilling to know that the
buyer of that plow is going to sell it to your brother
for twenty dollars. Old Billy Carter said, "Something's worth what someone will pay for it." He's
right. You got to feel good when a scoutmaster pays
good cash for a seventy-eight rpm record of "T for
Texas" or "Chattanooga Choo Choo," songs that
never should have been written in the first place. Boy
Scouts should have as their motto "Semper Eme;

Semper Vende," "always buy; always sell." They
should be taught that if you want to do good to your
neighbor you should buy his junk. And sell it for a
profit to the next generation of Scouts.

It was during the reading of the want ads in the *Kansan Newspaper* on Wednesday, May 9, 1984, that I realized that Skyblue was in town or had been. Kitty
Carbuncle, who comes to visit me each Friday afternoon and brings me Barnum's Animals Crackers that
I can soak up in my mouth and gum away without
the pain of false teeth, told me two weeks ago that
the old pasture on Ben Kitzler's old farm had been
sold. She lives next door to Dick Allbaugh, who runs
the Allbaugh Realty. He told her to tell me that the
pasture had been sold to an anonymous buyer on
January 9. Why he thought I'd be interested I don't
know. Kitty told me, anyway, and said, "You don't
suppose it was Skyblue who bought it?" I said, "Of
course not. He's not that stupid. The dirt in that
pasture won't even grow weeds. It should be used
for fill." I forgot about the sale although it did occur to me that the date of purchase was Skyblue's
fifty-fourth birthday.

On Wednesday, there was the ad. It read:
"Wanted: Wrought-iron railings and wrought-iron
grave crosses — not stolen from Ellis County." At
first I was furious. It got my dander up because I
knew some historian was sending a message to some
hick to go out and steal some of that stuff and he'd
buy it and preserve it for posterity. That's usually the
reason for their theft. High, noble ideals that moti-

vate crime. It's historians who steal stone fence posts, stained-glass doors and windows, religious scrolls, Rosetta stones, obelisks, the Elgin marbles. I'm surprised the pyramids are not in London or Paris. Probably they are too heavy to cart away. The next day the ad about the wrought-iron railings and crosses had disappeared from the paper and I knew the evil had been done.

When my anger had cooled down, I remembered that there was something else. I knew there was a third piece to be added. I lay in my darkness all Wednesday evening, all day Thursday and all Thursday evening and tried to recall it. I hid my sleeping pills so I could stay awake and think. Yosemite Sam, the night attendant, came in late Thursday night and I held his hand in the dark, as I often do, while he told me that his no-good son had flunked English again. When he left, it came to me. It was the obituary in the *Kansan* on Tuesday, May 8. It was the obituary that I didn't listen to closely because something was under my upper plate. It was the obituary, read because Quasimodo demanded it, of LaDonna Magdalene Kitzler, the daughter of Ben "Dirtbrown" Kitzler and the niece of Peter Seiltanzer, a.k.a., Skyblue the Badass. I knew that Skyblue had supported LaDonna for years in Wheatfield Acres, a holding pen for retarded adults, a place to put them until they could no longer live. I remembered that LaDonna went bad May 7, 1984. She was forty-two years old and had been in Wheatfield Acres for twenty-five years. Everything fell into place. I realized that Skyblue had purchased the pasture and was going to bury LaDonna in it. I didn't expect the rest.

Early this morning, I ordered Clutch Cargo, our physical therapy director, to load me in my wheel-chair and take me to a telephone. He had to do it be-cause we're allowed one phone call a day. If we make more than one phone call per day, we get no paper hats and no noisemakers at our birthday celebrat-tions. Clutch loaded me. He dialed and I talked to Kitty. She said she'd figured it all out on Wednesday. She said she'd check things out and tell me about them when she came for her usual Friday afternoon visit. I said, "Don't worry about the animal crackers." And she hung up.

It was my longest Friday as I waited for Kitty to arrive. When she finally did come late this after-noon, it was all over. She said that after she talked to me this morning, she started up her Model-A and drove out to the old pasture on Ben's old farm. On the top of the small hill by Middle Emma Creek there was a burial plot surrounded by wrought-iron rail-ings, a square plot with two marked graves and two laid-out plots. I was relieved to hear that the two marked graves had granite headstones. The head-stones were at the west end of the graves. The stone on the grave farthest to the north was for Agatha Theresa, Skyblue's sister who died in 1976 and was cremated in Wichita, she being the first to leave us. The next grave was LaDonna's, the second to go away. Next came a plot for Ben. It was marked with a small wooden cross with his name on it. Then an unmarked plot. The whole family would lie in that plot surrounded by wrought-iron fencing on the top of that hill.

Kitty said that when she returned from the pasture, she went to Chilblain Street to see Ben. He was asleep on the dirty couch in his dirty bib overalls. When Kitty got him awake, he told her that Skyblue was in Newton and was staying at the Red Coach Inn. Ben said that Skyblue had arranged everything. He had paid for the funeral. That he had hired a pickup truck and had come sometime Wednesday night to the old house on Chilblain Street. That he had scooped out and hauled away all the dirt in the petunia bed where Agatha's ashes had been dumped. That he had hauled the dirt out to the pasture and buried it and marked the grave with a headstone. Kitty asked Ben how Skyblue looked and Ben said he didn't know because he had only talked to him on the phone. When Kitty called the Red Coach Inn, Skyblue had already checked out and returned to Cincinnati and my last chance to see him had passed me by.

Kitty and I sat in the late Friday afternoon silence, me in my darkness and she in her glow, until she began to tell again, as she does every Friday, how Skyblue came to her first grade class at Ferdinand Elementary. She told again of his blond hair, his blue eyes. How thin he was. How he sat straight on the highest green chair under the Wandering Jew and smiled as the words came to him. Smiled at "See Dick run" and "Run, Spot, run." Told again how she followed his fortunes all the days of his life. Things read in newspapers, things heard on the street, gossip in the beauty parlor, calls to Ben Kitzler if he was sober, letters written to direct the care of LaDonna, chats with me. Recalled her visit to Cincinnati to see him. Recalled how she and I met, by chance, on the bus from Cincinnati to Louisville where we were both going to see the Kentucky Derby. How we both missed him in Cincinnati. How we have not seen him in almost forty years and would never see him again. Kitty recalled in her sniffling what had been her life — probably for the last time. Recalled what had been her order and her reason — probably for the last time.

It broke my heart to hear Kitty sniffle. It broke my heart to know that all she had to hold onto in her last days was the memory of one first grader out of the thousand or so she must have had in her class at Ferdinand Elementary. She told me once that she began teaching there when she was twenty and taught until she was seventy. She walked the two blocks to the school each day. She never missed a day in those fifty years. Never courting. Never marrying. Never carousing. Never traveling beyond the city limits until she decided to see the Kentucky Derby before she passed on, not having anything else to do with her savings. Never complaining about her brother who drove his new Buicks onto Nagol Street and parked so the little girls could climb on his lap, call him "Uncle Rosco" and kiss him for Chiclets. Never complaining about the Depression, World War II,

Korea, Viet Nam. Teaching Sunday School at the Presbyterian Church. Attending worship services. Never raising a flag or buying a war bond. Never marching in a parade. Reading her Bible and nursery rhymes. Fairy tales and *Dick and Jane* until she became like what she read and who she taught. Was never called Katherine until a Christmas card in 1936 from the blond boy on the high green chair, the card addressed to Miss Katherine Anne Carbuncle. Which she never forgot and whom she never forgot although she only knew about him by chance in the rest of his life. He and his life substituting for all that was never there and she never even seeing him, probably still thinking of him as he was when he was six years old and reading "There was a man of double deed," "In Winter I get up at night" and "I will begin the story of my adventures with a certain morning early in the month of June, the year of grace 1751, when I took the key for the last time out of the door of my father's house." Stupid of me to mind the sniffling. My twelve years of darkness have made me intolerant.

In our last colloquy, I recalled how I lived next door to him. How in 1936 I could not get out of bed one day and banged my cane against the wall until someone knocked on the door and said, "May I come in, Mr. Weary?" And I said, "You bet." And he said, "I'm Peter Seiltanzer, your neighbor. People call me Skyblue. I'm a first grader. Do you need some help?" I needed help and he helped. Every day of my life for ten years he came to take care of me. To wash me.

To feed me. To read to me. Until he was sixteen and drifted away.

I recalled how I missed him when he started going out to Ben Kitzler's farm when Ben married Agatha Theresa, Skyblue's sister. How I missed him while he stayed out on that burnt-up farm and kept Agatha company while Ben played punchboards and drank cheap wine. How I missed him when my little house got cold and there was no one to build a fire for me. When he returned home, he would come immediately to see me and scold me as if I were a child. He'd say things like, "Mr. Weary, why haven't you changed your sheets for a week?" He'd say, "You've got to eat properly to keep up your strength" and "Why haven't you used the bedpan, for heaven's sake?" Usually it took him all morning to get me cleaned up. It took two days to get my bedding washed out and my clothes clean again. How I missed him when he went off to college and became a professor of English at the University of Cincinnati. I missed him especially when Ben told me that Skyblue'd become a president and had his own secretary. I asked what he was president of and Ben said he supposed it was the university.

I especially remember, whenever Kitty Carbuncle comes to visit me, how I went to Cincinnati to see him in May of 1969. Fifteen years ago now. I wanted to see the Kentucky Derby before I lost my eyesight completely. By way of Cincinnati to Louisville just to see him. I remember how the cab driver helped me up the fourteen stairs to his apartment on Riddle

Road. How I waited for twelve hours, but he did not come home. I never told Ben or Kitty what a mess Skyblue's apartment was. How I returned to the bus and headed for Louisville to see the Derby the next day. How I met Kitty on the bus, not having known her before even though we had both lived in Newton for more than sixty years. There she first told me about him being in her first grade class at Ferdinand Elementary. How he blossomed with the written word. How Kitty and I got a room together in the Holiday Inn, got drunk on Old Grand-Dad, and never saw Churchill Downs, never saw Majestic Prince win the Derby because we were asleep, fully clothed, in a bed together. The trip was for both of us a pathetic gesture to bring back something we could never know again.

I have waited these thirty-eight years for him to come back, but he has not and now I can't see him again. I have waited all these years for him to come back and roll me over in my bed so my bedsores can heal. I've waited for him to come again and wash me and run my errands. I've waited mostly for him to come back again and read to me. At night, when all I can hear is Btfstlk calling out, "Will someone help me, please?" and Gravel Gertie is snoring over her rubber doll and King David is kneeling by his bed and praying aloud for the Second Coming, I think, in the noisy darkness, of Nagol Street and the neighbor boy who came smiling into my darkened room and read me the Bible, the *Evening Kansan Republican*, Hesiod's *Works and Days*, "The Tempest," *Great Expectations* and *The Sun is my Un-doing*. I recall him stumbling on words like "nicti-tating," "Ahithophel," "stertorous," "magnanimous," "Lenaion" and "Thalarctos maritimus." I remember his shivering in the cold and his sweating in the heat. I remember the smell of his breath, the gold in his fillings, the blond down on his chin and cheeks, the blond eyebrows moving with the sentences, the thin-ness of his arms, the softness of his fingernails. I remember him wiggling his ears to make me laugh when Mr. Jingle spoke Kansan instead of Cockney.

At 9:00 each night, Porkie Pig comes around and gives us our sleeping pills. I take the two pills, pre-tend to swallow them, drink a little water and say, "Good night, Miss Pharmacopoeia. Good night." She always giggles and says, "You're cute, William Weary. Real cute." I hide the pills under my pillow so that I can flush them down the toilet the next morning. Once Scorchy Smith caught me doing it. He said, "Willie, if you don't take those pills I'll re-port you to Catherine the Great and you'll get no aid to help you play Bingo." I said, "She's not paying for them." Scorchy said, "You're funny, Willie. Real funny." I bet I am. Because I don't want to sleep. Even if it means holding Yosemite Sam's hand and listening to him tell how his rotten son flunked So-cial Studies. In a few more months, days, hours, may-be even minutes or seconds, I will go bad and I will sleep forever. I want to lie in my darkness and re-member because in my last days what was furthest away is most near. In my last days I want to relive

what I missed in my crippled, supine life. I lie in the
darkness and listen to Joe Btfstlk cry out, "Will
someone help me, please?" I listen to the snoring,
the choking, the belching, Yosemite Sam. The TV
sets finally off. The floor waxing machines finally
shut down. I hear King David calling out for the
Second Coming. I hear my life running out of my
catheter. I lie in the west wing, north side, of Howdy
Doody Villa and await the pale stranger.

I know it is daytime here when Yosemite Sam says
good morning to all the domiciles in the west wing
and goes home to punish his failing issue. I know it
is morning when Punjab lifts me and washes me and
dresses me. I know it is morning when Porkie Pig
shaves me with an electric razor, running her fingers
over my facial skin to find the missed bristles. Dr.
Buffalo Bob comes with his cheery voice and digs the
feces out of my anus. They all laugh and call us the
Seven Dwarfs, Cabbage Patch, Smurf, Gravel Gertie and Wee Willie. When Clutch Cargo comes to
bend my legs, fingers, toes, arms, neck, I say to him,
"Let me go. I've had enough. The only way out of
this bed is to go bad. I'm ready." Clutch says, "Wee
Willie, you're a comedian. You know that? A real
comedian." And I'm not laughing.

I know it is nighttime when the ward becomes
filled with snoring and the screaming dreams of the
poor in spirit. I know it is night time when Yosemite
Sam comes in and sits down by my bed. He knows I
lie awake, trying to know the last minutes of my
existence. He knows I fight off sleep because soon I

will sleep forever. Because he knows and because he knows I know he knows, I reach out my right hand. He holds it because he knows my darkness and because he knows that I know he has his darkness too. He says, "Willie, my boy flunked math again. I don't know what I'm going to do with him. Looks like he'll never amout to nothing." And I say, "Can he see?" Sam says, "Of course he can see." I say, "Everybody amounts to something."

When Yosemite Sam has gone away from me and when my thoughts of going bad become too monotonous, I have a favorite fantasy that lifts my heart. It is a fantasy of how I won't go bad. It's wonderful to lie in my bed, think about the past and know that out on the expressways the finger of God is flicking bodies into eternity just as, as a child, I used to shoot marbles out of a circle in the dust. Cadillac, flick. Buick, flick. Dodge, flick. "Mommy, look at the pretty cow. Where, sweetie pie? Good God. Where'd that semi come from?" Squealing tires. Blood. Bodies. Broken glass. Burning gasoline. Wonderful thoughts; wonderful bed. Jesus, it's sweet to lie here. Fifty thousand and more a year. Flicked off like dandruff off the shoulder of a coat. Bodies off the shoulder of the road. Quickly cleaned up and covered up. The junk removed. Glass swept up. Very efficient. A whole industry. Make room for more. Bodies flying off the road and up to Jesus. Drivers and passengers need soulbelts not seatbelts because their severed asses are bleeding on the berm. Death traps from Detroit. Self-genocide. Slow, systematic elimination of a racial group marked by a congenital deformity called a Chrysler. I can see Jesus sitting at the right-hand of God and saying, "Come on, Dad. Can't you be a little quieter?" I smile and realize that that's one death every 105 seconds, one death every minute and forty-five seconds. That's in a slow year. Say, fifty-five miles per hour. At sixty, seventy, eighty, ninety. Tear down the speed limit signs; make narrow the lanes. In the monotony, I am cute. I am funny. I am a comedian.

When death comes for me I know I will see again and I know what I will see after this long dark night of waiting. Death will be a twelve year old boy knocking on my door. He will say, "May I come in?" And I will say, "You bet." He will open the white door. The morning light will be blinding. He will be almost six feet tall and very skinny. He will have been told by his mother that if he stands sideways to the sun he will cast no shadow. He will have blond hair, blond eyebrows and blue eyes. His gold fillings in his front teeth will glitter through his smile. Behind him, the tumultuous snows of the blizzard. As he enters, terrible cold winds will rake in the snow and I will shiver. He will close the door, stomp the snow from his black cowboy boots and remove his sheepskin coat and his purple knitted stocking cap. He will take the bottle of Old Grand-Dad off the chair and put it on the window sill. He will smooth my covers and then go to the kitchen to fry me two eggs, sunnyside up, make two pieces of toast from Wonder Bread. He will bring the breakfast to my bed and feed me, sopping the yolks into the toast. He will make a cup of hot Postum and hold it to my lips for the sipping. He will remove my covers. Remove my pajamas. He will take the bedpan out from under the bed and help me onto it. While I defecate and urinate he will go into the kitchen and sing "Gott ist die Liebe." When I have finished, he will return with the toilet paper, wipe me clean, take the bedpan to the toilet, empty it, wash it and put it back under my bed. He will fetch the wash basin, fill it with cold water, bring a washrag and towel. And wash me, rolling me from side to side. My face, my ears, my armpits, my crotch, my anus, between my toes. While I shiver, he will remove my false teeth and wash them. He will lift my legs to bend them and exercise them. He will bend my arms and fingers to exercise them. Rub my back. Comb my hair. He will change my sheets, rolling me onto one dirty side and making the other side of the bed, then roll me onto the clean side, remove the dirty sheets and finish making the bed. He will put on me a clean pair of green pajamas to stop the shivering. He will bring me water and give me my pills. He will cover me up, draw up my chair, sit down beside the bed and read, "Marley was dead: to begin with. There is no doubt whatever about that."

When death reads, "And so, as Tiny Tim observed, God Bless Us, Every One!" and the story is over, he will lay down the book on the bedside table, step to my side and close my eyes with his left hand so that he will not die. He will uncover me, lift me in his

arms like God said He would do. He will carry me
out into the fierce Kansas Winter and comfort me
as God promised. He will rise from the earth and
carry me up into the fierce winds, up into the blinding whiteness of the roiling snow. Death will smile
down upon me in his arms. He will smile and wiggle
his ears to tell me not to be afraid.

When we reach the high mountain and the balm
of the heavens, death will put me down by still waters
and green pastures according to God's word. He will
take a basket and open it. He will put in my false
teeth. He will feed me ham salad sandwiches. He
will cut a watermelon and feed me little pieces with
a fork. There will be cold fried chicken and sliced
bananas in strawberry Jell-O. He will pour me a glass
of grape Kool-Aid and hold it to my trembling lips.
He will challenge me to a sack race or a wheelbarrow
race, drop-the-handkerchief or horseshoes. He will
say, "Which side of the cat has the most fur?" We
will laugh together at the answer. He will ask, "What
kind of horse sees as well backwards as forwards?"
We will giggle at the answer. He will murmur, "Who
makes it doesn't need it; who sells it doesn't want
it; who needs it doesn't know it. What is it?" When
I will not laugh at the answer, death will wiggle his
ears, clean up the food and dishes, close the basket,
ride home on his bicycle, and I will be alone in my
white sheets and green pajamas and I will cry out,
I will cry out into God's darkness, "Will someone
help me, please?"

I will cry out, "Will someone help us, please?" because now I see. Here in the darkness of Howdy Doody Villa I see just as surely as if I were on Mt. Pisgah and looking into the Promised Land. I see and know what will be for me and for Skyblue and his kin. For after Skyblue's interment, no one will go to the little cemetery on the hill by the Middle Emma Creek. The weeds and grass will grow very high inside the wrought-iron railings and the cattle will lean against the railings and push against them to get to the high grass inside. In a few years, the railings will be pushed over and the cattle will tromp on the graves. Weeds and grass will hide the wrought-iron railings that lie on the ground. The cattle will rub against the gravestones until they topple. Grass and weeds will grow over them too and soon they will disappear and no one will know what is there. Big yellow machines will arrive. A death-trap expressway will be built nearby. The hill in the old pasture will be leveled and used for fill dirt.

This book was designed and printed letter-press on Warren's Olde Style by Rosmarie Waldrop. The initial letters and offset cover are by Keith Waldrop. The cover uses a detail from "The Fairy Feller's Master Stroke" by Richard Dadd. The text was linotyped in 10 pt. Palatino by Mollohan Typesetting in West Warwick, RI. Smyth-sewn into paper covers by Bay State Bindery in Boston. There are 2000 copies, of which 50 are signed by the author.